Adve...

LÁSZLÓ HÁMORI

When fourteen-year-old Jan left Sweden at the end of the school year to join his parents in Bangkok, where his father was serving as an adviser to the Thailand airline, he had not expected to find a summer job. But Hans Nittel, the young hydraulic engineer Jan met on the flight out, who was in charge of drilling artesian wells in Thailand for the World Health Organization, offered him part-time work at the proposed site of the first well.

The work went smoothly at first; then unpleasant things began to happen. Who were the men who stole two of Hans's precious geological maps? Why was one of the packing cases containing Hans's drilling machinery redirected to Rangoon by a mysterious stranger? These were only some of the questions that confronted Jan and Hans—and their Thai friend and helper Snit. When Hans disappeared without a trace, it was the boys who finally stumbled on the meaning of these events and on the identity of the unscrupulous character behind it all.

Set in a colorful and complex land that is depicted in vivid detail, this is a rousing story of adventure and intrigue.

ADVENTURE IN BANGKOK

by the same author

DANGEROUS JOURNEY
FLIGHT TO THE PROMISED LAND

ADVENTURE IN BANGKOK

László Hámori

Translated from the Swedish by Annabelle MacMillan

Illustrated by Robert Frankenberg

HARCOURT, BRACE & WORLD, INC., NEW YORK

CONTENTS

1	A NARROW ESCAPE FROM DROWNING	9
2	JAN MAKES A MOVE	25
3	A LETTER AND A CHASE AFTER THIEVES	35
4	SNIT ENTERS THE PICTURE	51
5	A SHIP COMES LOADED	67
6	SCARFACE POPS UP AGAIN	81
7	DOG GOES INTO ACTION	98
8	THE DAILY ROUTINE AND A NEW MYSTERY	111
9	A LETTER AND NOTHING MORE	124
10	JOURNEY INTO THE UNKNOWN	143
11	A SURPRISE AND A VISIT	158
12	THE DRILLING MACHINERY RUNS AGAIN	176

ADVENTURE IN BANGKOK

Chapter One

❖❖❖❖

A NARROW ESCAPE FROM DROWNING

"Hans! Hans! Steer to the left!"

"What's the matter? What are you yelling about?"

"Look. Over there in the middle of the river. . . . Hurry up, Hans. Move, for heaven's sake!"

Hans needed no additional prodding. With one quick motion of his hand, he changed the monotonous putt-putt of the motor into an almost deafening roar, after which the motorboat headed at top speed in the direction Jan was pointing. Right in the middle of the mighty Menam Chao Phraya, the mother of all rivers according to the Thailand tradition, a long narrow boat was bobbing, bottom side up, in the yellowish water. Floating near the capsized craft were four gilded oars and a small bright red bundle, while two men splashed around desperately in an attempt to keep afloat.

While the motorboat raced toward the scene of the accident, Jan was removing his shirt and kicking off his sandals; he was down to his khaki-colored shorts. About twenty yards from the capsized boat, he made a graceful dive into the water. To the astonishment of his friend, however, he swam, not toward the two men who were flailing about wildly, but

straight toward the small red bundle. For a moment he was
hidden by a billowing wave, but a few seconds later Hans
sighted him again.

By then his free hand was holding the bright red bundle
above the water, and he was on his way back to the
motorboat, kicking violently. He didn't have far to go, because Hans in the meanwhile had brought the boat up closer
to him.

Clinging to the side of the boat with one hand, he lifted

the bundle up and said, breathlessly, "You take care of this. I can get up by myself."

While Jan struggled to get back into the boat, Hans cast an astonished glance at the sopping wet little bundle in the bottom of the boat.

"Good heavens, Jan, there's a little child in there!" he exclaimed in surprise.

"Yes, I know," Jan panted. "But now help me get him out of all these wrappings. On second thought, maybe it's best if you navigate, but steer over to shore as fast as you can. We don't have a second to lose. . . ."

The motor sputtered again as the boat swung off in a wide semicircle toward the left bank of the river. In the meantime, Jan loosened the full red silk robe, and from its folds emerged a little Chinese boy who looked to be about two and a half years old. Jan held the seemingly lifeless body in his arms; the delicate, slant-eyed face showed not the slightest sign of life.

"Hey, Jan," said Hans from his position at the tiller. "What are we going to do about the two men? Shouldn't we have tried to get them into the boat, too?"

"Oh, they can take care of themselves, I'm sure," Jan replied. "Both of them can swim by the looks of it, or for that matter, they can cling to the boat. But the boy had already gone under twice before I got there."

By this time the boat had reached the bank. Jan hurried ashore, holding the limp body of the small Chinese boy in his arms. With all possible speed, he laid the body face up on the ground and began giving him mouth-to-mouth artificial respiration. After dragging the prow of the boat up onto the land, Hans ran up with a blanket. Lifting up the child, they placed the blanket under him and continued their resuscitation attempts.

In a matter of minutes, a large group of curious onlookers had assembled—barefoot men in short pants, children of all shapes and sizes, and a few women in ankle-length skirts. They had come from the nearby houses and fishing huts or from their jobs; they were vastly interested, but their faces were expressionless as they watched Jan work with the small lifeless body. Apparently, they didn't like what they were seeing, because some of the women began to scream in protest, while the men talked among themselves in their strange guttural voices. A few of them stepped out of the group and moved threateningly toward Jan.

Hans stepped forward and, gesturing wildly, began to explain to them, which seemed to calm them somewhat. Even so, the circle pushed in still closer, and Jan, taking a moment's rest, begged Hans to try pushing the crowd back so that the child could get more air. Once more Hans began to speak to the crowd, but the results were meager. The onlookers wanted to be as close as possible to see what the young *farang,* or foreigner, was up to.

Jan began to tire. The sustained huffing and puffing had put a severe strain on his lungs and chest muscles. In addition, he could see no good resulting from his efforts. The small form still lay motionless, and its cheeks were just as pale as before. Now and then he alternated his mouth-to-mouth respiration with chest massage, which didn't seem to help either. It appeared to be completely impossible to get the boy to breathe again. Jan began to fear that he had arrived too late to save the child. Perspiration dripped from his forehead, both from anxiety and physical strain.

The barefoot men were beginning to be agitated again, and Hans had to shout at them at the top of his lungs to keep them from attacking Jan. Jan, however, was so absorbed in what he was doing and so worried about the child that he didn't seem to notice. He even seemed unaware that everything had suddenly quieted down—that the menacing, gesticulating men and the screaming women were now standing as if they had been paralyzed or struck dumb.

The closed circle began to widen, and a Chinese man in a gray chauffeur's uniform pushed his way through. Loudly and repeatedly, he shouted, "Make way! Make way for my master, Fu Man-Tsu." A few yards behind him followed a striking figure, walking with small, quick steps—Mr. Fu Man-Tsu himself.

Fu Man-Tsu was tall for a Chinese and as thin as a rail. Had he not been bent with age, he would have stood a head taller than anyone in the assemblage gathered around Jan. His spare figure was clad from throat to ankles in a billowing silk robe decorated with serpentine embroidery in red and gold. The elderly man—you could tell by his thin white beard that he must be very old—had a small golden cap on his head, on the crown of which was a crystal ball the size of an egg. Everything about him commanded respect—his figure, age, and dress.

The chauffeur in gray managed to push the crowd back a little. The elegantly dressed man came forward until he stood right beside Jan, who was still so absorbed in his efforts that he didn't even look up. And just as the old man bent his

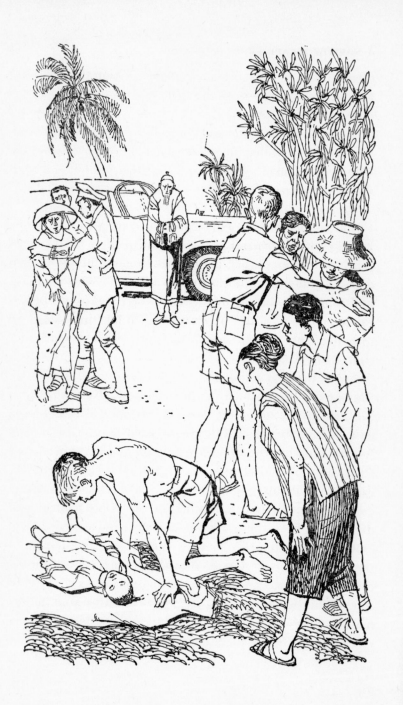

crooked back a little so that he could see better, a small but audible sound came from the little boy. It sounded like the meow of a cat.

"Move over, Hans," Jan commanded, raising his head. The result was that a second later he was looking the wrinkled old man right in the face. Fu Man-Tsu backed away a little, pointing his long, bony finger at the child.

"Continue," he ordered.

But Jan needed no admonition to continue. Cautiously, in time with the breathing, he began to press on the boy's chest. As the child began to breathe regularly, he whimpered occasionally. A few moments later he opened his coal-black eyes to the world, and the first thing he caught sight of was Fu Man-Tsu's bearded face. Stretching his little arms up toward the old man, he began to sob loudly, as he said in a thin voice, "A-ta, A-ta, A-ta."

Gently pushing Jan aside, the old Chinese man picked up the child. His uniformed chauffeur began to forge a path for him once more, and the old man pushed his way through the crowd carefully as if carrying a parcel of inestimable worth. As Jan arose, he could see, behind the crowd, a well-kept Chevrolet. Obviously, the old man had arrived in it. On each side of the dark blue car was painted a huge serpentine gold dragon—symbols, no doubt, of the owner's might and dignity.

Preceding him, the chauffeur opened the car door, and the elegantly dressed master got in, still holding the sobbing child in his arms. Quickly, the chauffeur slid into the driver's seat, and a few seconds later nothing remained where the car had stood but a cloud of dust.

The crowd began to disperse. People withdrew in small

groups, discussing, in both high shrill voices and heavy guttural tones, the exciting events they had just witnessed. A
few moments later Jan and Hans were alone on the shore.
They walked over to the motorboat, which Hans pushed out
into the water. While Jan got on board, Hans started the
motor. The boat swung into midstream, and soon they had
reached a high iron bridge, under which they tied up at a
little wooden pier and walked ashore. An attendant in
a white shirt and shorts helped them and transferred the boat
to a mooring bearing Hans's name.

Jan, who by this time had put on his shirt and sandals
again, and Hans took a small winding street leading from
the river toward the city. It was almost noon, and the sun
was beating down mercilessly across the conglomeration of
houses. Hans headed for an outdoor café and the shade of its
wide awning, with Jan tagging along behind.

As they poured an ice-cold Coca-Cola into their glasses on
the small table, Hans, after taking a great, huge gulp, said,
"Well, that's over and done with. But do you realize that we
might have gotten ourselves into some real trouble?"

"Real trouble?" Jan repeated in astonishment. "We didn't
do anything wrong! On the contrary, we saved the life of a
little Chinese boy."

"Right you are. But you're forgetting one thing. Once before I told you that the Thailanders don't like it when people touch them. The ones who have a good deal to do with
Europeans and Americans have gradually, but reluctantly,
gotten used to shaking hands, but two Thailanders would
never think of shaking hands with one another. And they
would be hard put to imagine anything more undignified
than a pat on the shoulder, even if the pat were accompanied

by the friendliest intentions in the world. There are a good many American soldiers who have gotten into difficulties simply because they insisted on friendly pats on the back. And fondling, petting, or, for that matter, even touching a small child is regarded as an insult, both to the child and to its parents."

"But I've never patted anyone on the shoulder or anywhere else!" Jan objected.

"Well, you certainly touched that little Chinese kid! The Thailanders had never seen the like of what you did—a young *farang* putting a child on the ground and blowing it full of air!"

"But this is ridiculous—all of it!" Jan said. "They must have seen that I was just trying to get the child to breathe again and . . ."

"Don't be too sure that they understood. But now, tell me how in the world you caught sight of the little boy in the water."

"When we started out from the big temple on the other side, I couldn't tear my eyes away from its fantastic tower. The little tiles on the sides of the tower caught the reflection of the sun so brilliantly that I was almost blinded, so I finally had to turn my face away. And just as I did that, I noticed a long narrow boat floating along in the river. It was painted red, and on the stem was a golden dragon head. Two men, standing up, were rowing, but as a tugboat came chugging by, they lost control of the craft and fell into the water. To be truthful, I don't know myself if I caught a glimpse of the boy's head or if it was pure instinct that told me there was a small child in the red bundle."

"Well, no matter which way it was, it was a lucky thing for

the youngster that your eyes are so sharp and your instincts
so dependable," Hans said, ending the conversation. After he
paid for the Coca-Cola, both the young *farangs* left the cool
shade of the awning. As they were about to go their
own ways, Jan happened to think of something.

"Who do you suppose that bearded Chinese was, anyway?
I mean the one that came after the child."

"I have no idea," Hans replied. "But he didn't seem to be
very poverty-stricken. Chauffeur, Chevrolet, a gold-em-
broidered robe . . ."

"Oh, I'm positive he's rich, but he didn't seem to be especially grateful. I don't think it would have hurt him to say
thank you at least. And it certainly would be interesting to
know who he is."

As early as that very evening, Jan's questions were
answered while he was eating dinner with his parents on the
terrace of their home. During dessert—ice-cold mangoes
served by a boy in white—he told his parents of his morning
adventure. His father listened attentively, whistling in
amazement as Jan spoke of the chauffeur who had cried,
"Make way! Make way for my master, Fu Man-Tsu."

"Well, I'm astonished!" his father said. "Don't you know
who you met, my boy? Haven't you ever heard of the
Mandarin Fu Man-Tsu?"

"Mandarin? Do they call him that because he sells
mandarin oranges or because his skin is yellowish?"

"Don't be silly! You certainly ought to know that
'Mandarin' is a title of honor from the time that China was
an empire, bestowed on those who passed a very difficult
examination in Chinese. If they desired, these Mandarins
—the closest thing to our Doctor of Philosophy degree—were

given high state positions after passing the examination. But Fu Man-Tsu has never held such a position in China. He himself, his father, his grandfather, and his great-grandfather were all born here in Thailand. The Fus have always been a noble and wealthy family, and in line with his father's wishes, this Fu Man-Tsu as a young man studied in China. After he had passed his examination and won the right to wear a crystal ball on his cap, he returned to Bangkok and took over as director of the family enterprise."

"What sort of family enterprise was this?"

"Was? They still have it. But what the enterprise deals with isn't so easy to explain in a few words. The family owns a whole group of rice mills all over the country, and they own the country's largest bank, which is patronized by most of the Chinese who live here in Thailand. The Fu family business exports a considerable part of the country's most important products—rice and teakwood. In addition, the family owns at least fifty or so opium cafés."

"Opium cafés? Places where people smoke opium, you mean? But opium is a narcotic, and narcotic traffic is forbidden the world over," the wide-eyed Jan objected.

"The world over in theory, but not really in Thailand. Here in Bangkok, opium dens are more or less sanctioned, and I don't exaggerate at all when I say they are flourishing. Many of the Chinese in this country smoke two or three pipefuls a day. But to get back to Fu Man-Tsu, I can tell you that he is not only the wealthiest of all the Chinese in Thailand but also their leader here. He is the president of the organization called the Golden Dragon."

"And what's that, anyway?"

"It's a secret Chinese society, and secret societies exist any-

where in the world where the Chinese are found. A number
of them were founded originally in China over a thousand
years ago. In the beginning, they had religious connections,
but little by little they have enlarged their scope. Most of
them indulge in charity work and support the members
who have gotten into difficulties. Some of them exist for political purposes as well. It isn't easy to find out much about
them because the members are sworn to silence. Here in
Thailand, the Golden Dragon is the strongest and wealthiest
of these societies, and, as I explained, Fu Man-Tsu is the
president of it."

"Well, I can see that's he's a prominent man. But what
does he have to do with the little boy who was about to
drown?"

"The boy's name is Ho-Chin, and he is Fu Man-Tsu's
great-grandson. They say around town that the old man has
chosen him as his sole heir. When Fu Man-Tsu dies, little
Ho-Chin will inherit all his millions as well as the presidency
of the Golden Dragon. But he has lots of time to grow to
manhood before this happens. Fu Man-Tsu is only eighty-
three, you see."

"*Only* eighty-three?" Jan repeated with a grin.

"Don't laugh, Jan. All of Bangkok's Chinese know that
Fu Man-Tsu has made up his mind to live until he is one
hundred and two. One hundred and two, you see, is some
sort of magic number to the Chinese. And they say, too, that
Fu Man-Tsu heretofore has always done exactly as he
decided and promised . . ."

"Thank you, Father. Thanks for all the information,
which really was interesting. But I wonder if you can tell me,

then, why this eminent, famous Fu Man-Tsu didn't even mutter as much as a thank you after I had saved his heir from drowning? You know perfectly well that I didn't rescue the kid just to be thanked, but I think it's very peculiar. Don't you?"

"To be truthful, I don't understand it at all. Chinese people, and especially the older, more educated classes among them, are the most courteous in the world. But some day maybe we'll find out why the Mandarin didn't observe even the most elementary rules of etiquette."

That riddle was solved, too—bright and early the next morning. The Grundvahl family was eating breakfast on the veranda when the servant boy came to inform them that a Chinese man had arrived and wanted to speak with Mr. Grundvahl. The Chinese, when he was shown in, was attired in white European-style clothing and wore glasses on the end of his nose. He introduced himself as Fu Man-Tsu's private secretary. After a brief exchange of words, he took out a note, rolled in a yellow silk cloth, and written in flawless English.

"Highly esteemed Sir Engineer! Yesterday was a day when the stars and constellations were highly unfavorable for me. On the way to my home, my great-grandson Ho-Chin was very nearly the victim of a fatal accident as he was being rowed across the river, and all because of the great carelessness of my servants. Fortunately, of course, his life was saved, but since all this took place on an unfavorable day, I felt it was not proper to turn my attention to you at once.

"Today the constellations are looking upon me with favor, which is why I allow myself now to express my gratitude to

you. You will have to bear with my scanty knowledge of the
English language, which may result in my not finding the
proper expressions for making this feeling of gratefulness
known to you. Have patience, therefore, with an ignorant,
elderly man. I can only say that as long as I live I will never
be able to pay my indebtedness to you and that I will forever
feel obliged to you.

"I would consider it a great honor, indeed, if I might at
any time be of service to you yourself or to a member of your
honored family, whatever that service might be. In the hope
of making a slight attempt at relieving my indebtedness, I
would like, through my secretary, to give you a piece of trivia
as a completely inadequate token of my thankfulness.

"Your most humble and forever grateful servant,

Fu Man-Tsu"

After he had read the text, written on yellow silk with red
India ink, the secretary, with a deep bow, handed flight
Engineer Grundvahl a miniature boat, and from the boat
he took a small case of shining, almost transparent green
jade. The case was intricately carved on all sides, and Mr.
Grundvahl realized immediately that he was holding in his
hands a masterpiece of Chinese craftsmanship.

After an additional ceremony of deep bowing, the secretary took leave. Utterly delighted, the Grundvahl family
studied the marvelous jade case, which they had placed in
the middle of the table, and all of a sudden Mrs. Grundvahl
hit upon the idea that it might possibly open. No more than
the slight pressure of a fingertip was needed to get it open.
And inside was a fired ceramic figure about four inches tall

—a horse with a tall rider. Cautiously, Mr. Grundvahl picked up the small horse.

"A good-luck piece from the Ming Dynasty," he declared. "Five or six hundred years ago the Chinese used to place things of this sort in graves as burial gifts. Nowadays they are considered rarities in the larger European and American museums. Fu Man-Tsu has truly shown his gratitude with a princely gift like this."

"Oh, sure. The case is beautiful, and the horse is really very nice," Jan exclaimed. "But what I don't understand is why the old Mandarin is thanking you and sending presents to you for something that I did," he added somewhat resentfully.

"You have no reason to feel that you have been put aside or to be resentful of Fu Man-Tsu," his father said consolingly. "All over the Far East, this is the way they do things. When a member of a family does something honorable or worthy of praise, all the honor is bestowed on the head of the family. In earlier times, when a soldier did something heroic on the battlefield, the Emperor never honored the soldier himself but instead honored his father. Even as late as World War II, the Emperor of Japan didn't bestow honors on soldiers but on their fathers. And since I happen to be your father and the head of our family, the old Mandarin has thanked me because you saved Ho-Chin's life, and this is the reason he has sent the present to me."

"That's all well and good," Jan answered, not at all content with his father's explanation. "But I think it might have occurred to the old Chinaman that we aren't Orientals. We're Swedes. Scandinavians. Europeans."

"Take it easy, Jan," Flight Engineer Grundvahl said with
a laugh. "There's no question that the present is yours, and
no one is going to try to take it away from you. You were the
one who managed to rescue the Mandarin's great-grandson
from the river."

Chapter Two

❖❖❖

JAN MAKES A MOVE

Jan, whose full name was Jan-Eric Grundvahl, was a typical Swedish boy. He had medium blond hair, blue eyes, and an oval face. In addition, he was a passionate ice-hockey player and a jazz enthusiast. He swam well and, as a rule, was not much for serious studying in school, but he read the comics regularly. He had just finished the eighth grade of an elementary school in suburban Stockholm.

He was still in the eighth grade in Sweden when this story really began—with a conversation between the head of the personnel department of Scandinavian Airlines System and Flight Engineer Jan-Eric Grundvahl, Senior, Jan's father. Mr. Grundvahl was an employee of Scandinavian Airlines, and the personnel manager informed him that the Thai Airway International Company, which worked closely with SAS, was looking for an experienced flight engineer. And since experienced flight engineers don't exactly grow on trees in Thailand, they had asked SAS to loan them one for a period of two years. It seemed to the head of the personnel department that Flight Engineer Grundvahl was just the right man for the position in Thailand.

Four weeks later, at the end of October, the Grundvahl family took off for Thailand, but without Jan. In spite of his vigorous protests, his parents had decided that for the time being he would remain at home—or, rather, in Stockholm with his Aunt Britta, a charming relative who, actually, was Mrs. Grundvahl's aunt. She had a large apartment in the eastern part of the city. It was chiefly Mrs. Grundvahl who was responsible for this discouraging decision. She pointed out in the first place that Jan had been sick the previous year and that the difficult climate in Thailand would certainly not do him any good. Also—and this was her clinching argument—she reminded them that Jan had done far from brilliantly in school. Both parents were completely agreed that the loss of a whole year in school would be too high a price to pay for a trip to Thailand.

Deeply wounded, Jan had finally accepted the inevitable. His pain was eased somewhat by the knowledge that Mr. and Mrs. Grundvahl were just to fly to Bangkok and take a look at the situation, and that they might well be back in Sweden within a month. Furthermore, Father had shaken hands on a promise that, if they stayed in Bangkok, Jan could come to Thailand later on, provided that he passed the eighth grade with high marks.

Thus it was that Flight Engineer Grundvahl and his wife flew to Bangkok, the capital of Thailand, while Jan stayed with Aunt Britta. From November until June the correspondence between Bangkok and Stockholm was enormous. The Grundvahls gave detailed accounts of the way of life in the distant capital of Thailand, and Jan, in turn, kept his parents up to date on the weather in Sweden, the movies and television programs he had seen of late, and, sporadically, how things were going at school.

Jan wrote his last letter after examination day and was able to tell his parents, with more than a little pride, that he had made some pretty good grades: nothing but B's (disregarding a B-minus of course) and an A-minus in English. Also, that he had obeyed Aunt Britta, had let all her preachments serve as a guide to his behavior, and had eaten everything his nice aunt had put on his plate—a monumental amount of food.

Jan also mentioned that he had spoken with his class advisor, who had said that Jan could very easily go to Bangkok for a year without losing any time in school, provided that he read omnivorously while there. Naturally, he would have to enter the tenth grade on trial when he returned home. The doctor who had examined Jan was quick to say that Jan had grown appreciably stronger during the past year and that there was no·danger in his joining his parents.

One beautiful sunny day in June, then, Jan stood outside at Årlanda Airport, ready to climb aboard an SAS Coronado plane. There was no doubt that he was smitten with travel fever. To be sure, this was far from his first flight—he was the son of a flight engineer. Yet this very long trip, which he had to undertake all by himself, was making him slightly nervous. Soon the huge Coronado was aloft, soaring with such an easy sureness that even the most nervous of the passengers calmed down. Very quickly Jan was able to give the trip his undivided attention—as they flew first to Kastrup, Copenhagen's airport, and then on to Frankfurt-am-Main.

Up to the time they reached Frankfurt, Jan had been sitting alone, but here he was joined by a young man of medium height, wearing a sport jacket and slacks, who had a very winning smile. For a while, however, Jan had no time for his companion, because soon after take-off from Frankfurt the plane was over the Alps. Fortunately, the weather was sunny and clear, and there was a charming view through the oval window. The peaks of the Alps, over ten thousand feet high, were covered with glittering snow, which reflected the light of the sun. The small winding valleys between the wildly romantic mountains were emerald green, and here and there you could see the silvery course of a mountain river.

After a while Jan and his seat companion began to talk. In no time Jan found out that the young man with the smile was an Austrian, that his name was Hans Nittel, and that he was an engineer by profession, specializing in the digging of wells. The engineer, who had a relaxed manner in conversation, said that he had already spent three months in Thailand in the vicinity of the capital and that he had been back to Europe a couple of times to purchase tools and instruments, which he needed in connection with the wells.

Little by little, Hans Nittel and Jan felt so relaxed with one another that the engineer suggested Jan call him by his first name. They spoke in English—the one with a soft Austrian accent and the other with a somewhat more harsh Swedish accent—but they understood each other perfectly. Jan began to admit to himself that, when you came right down to it, his father had been right with his constant remarks back home that "There's no way around it. You've just got to have command of English."

Hans spoke a good deal about how he had come to be in Thailand. After he had gotten his engineer's license, he had

begun to work for an Austrian firm. But since he had always
longed to see the world and, at the same time, wished very
much to make his contribution in the underdeveloped countries, he read the want-ads regularly, especially those offering
jobs in exotic lands. One day he had seen an advertisement
in one of his professional magazines, stating that WHO, the
World Health Organization, was seeking an engineer for
digging artesian wells in Thailand. Immediately he applied
for and got the job.

"But I don't understand this," Jan said, interrupting him.
He was very skilled at raising questions about anything and
everything. "If I remember correctly, Bangkok is situated at
the mouth of a huge river, Menam Chao Phraya. And cities
on rivers don't generally need deep wells."

"A very good observation," Hans replied. "But I don't
think you have any idea of the extent to which the Thailanders who live beside the river use and misuse its waters. For
centuries now, they have dug thousands upon thousands of
canals for the purpose of irrigating and inundating the rice
fields. When the water is no longer needed on the rice fields,
the musty and polluted water of the canals is shunted back
into the river again. Moreover, the river serves not only as a
means of communication and place of bathing for the population but also as the main channel of garbage disposal. By
the same token, it is just as natural for a Thailander to obey
the call of nature in the river as it is for him to throw all sorts
of debris, including animal corpses and any sort of trash you
can think of, directly into it. Before the water reaches Bangkok, it has taken on about the same color as sewer water, and
heaven knows, it differs very little from sewer water in com-
position. To top it all, after the rainy season, masses of sand

and gravel from the mountainous districts to the north
make their way into the water. And then the inhabitants
of the city—half a million of them—drink this same water."

"But aren't there any purification plants in Bangkok,
then?" Jan asked.

"Naturally they have tried to filter and purify the water,
but they have had no success. Menam's water is so polluted
and impure that no amount of filtering in the world could
purify it again. And even if you were able to rid the water of
all its dangerous bacteria, you would have to use so much
chlorine that the water would be unfit for human consumption. That's the reason Thailand needs artesian wells that
can produce clean, clear water. Wells of this type can save
thousands of human lives as well as protect the population
against a whole lot of dreadful diseases, among them the
appalling infection called cholera."

When Hans saw the worried look on Jan's face, he added,
"Don't worry about it, boy. You won't die of cholera or ty-
phoid over there. Both the Caucasians and the wealthier of
the Thailanders have nothing to do with the river water. You
can buy any number of soft drinks in hygienic bottles. Clean
well water is for sale almost everywhere, and the breweries
manufacture beer and ale of all types."

By the time the plane landed in Karachi, the capital of
Pakistan, Hans had had time to initiate Jan into many of the
mysteries surrounding the digging of wells. The World
Health Organization had assigned the Austrian expert to
dig eight wells on the outskirts of Bangkok. Some of them
were to be the so-called "artesian" type. The designation
"artesian" comes from the first well of that sort dug in the
province of Artois in France. The principle behind an arte-

sian well is that one drill appreciably below the subsoil water level, continuing down to a subterranean water
deposit, which, by its own force, presses up toward the surface of the earth.

Hans explained to Jan that among the different earth
strata are some that do not at all, or to a very slight extent
only, allow water to pass through. In the interior of the earth
are cavities that lie between two such layers, and sometimes
these cavities are filled by water seeping in from the side or
from some sort of opening in the upper layer. The water
trapped between two such impassable layers is exposed to
tremendous pressure both from above and below. And if
you drill down to the entrapped water, it will erupt because
of the pressure, often forming a geyser fifty feet high.

Hans went on to say that the water in these artesian wells
is crystal clear and completely free of pollution, while the
subsoil water in many cases, as in Bangkok, is strongly polluted, even several yards beneath the earth's surface.

"Well, it all seems very simple to me," Jan said jokingly.
"It's just a matter of knowing where these deposits of water
are trapped and then drilling down to reach them so that
they erupt all by themselves."

"That's about it," Hans said laughingly. "It is just a matter of knowing where they are, and the drilling can get under
way at once. The only catch is that often you have to drill
pretty deep. Artesian wells of a depth of a thousand or
thirteen hundred feet are only small holes in the ground
when you think, for example, of the well in Sperenberg outside Berlin. That water comes from more than thirty-nine
hundred feet below the surface."

"Is that really true?" Jan said in amazement.

"Yes, it's true. But that sort of well is child's play in com-
parison to oil wells, where you often must drill to a depth
of ten thousand feet before you find the precious oil."

Hans mentioned that geologists had already made the
necessary surveys in the vicinity of Bangkok. The detailed
maps they had made showed the various layers of the earth
and their thicknesses and were now rolled up in aluminum
foil in a big cabinet in Hans's workroom. The Austrian engineer's assignment now was to supervise the work of the
surveyors on the job and, finally, to decide where the drilling
was to be done. That being accomplished, the master driller
could come and start work.

Jan, fascinated by the subject of well-drilling, asked if he
might pay Hans a visit at work. The first week after his arrival in Bangkok, he began going out to see Hans almost
every day. At home he mentioned his friend and the work
he was doing in the field so often that at length Mrs.
Grundvahl told her son to bring Hans home for dinner so
that the whole family could get to know him. In no time they
were all good friends.

One evening, while the servant Sharikat gave them coffee
on the terrace, Hans said to Mr. Grundvahl, "As you know,
Jan has been out most afternoons helping me with my
work . . ."

"Yes, I'm very much aware of the fact. He is probably
such a nuisance to you that you're going to put in a claim for
your lost working time, I would guess," Mr. Grundvahl replied.

"Oh, absolutely not. On the contrary, he is a conscientious
and good co-worker. As a matter of fact, I was about to make
you a proposition along that line. What I'd like to do is hire

Jan as a half-time apprentice. The funds they have allotted to me for this project cover such expenses, but of course I can't offer him an astronomical salary. The most I can offer is twelve dollars a week for twenty hours of work."

Mr. Grundvahl took a swallow of coffee before answering, and this brief pause was just enough time for Jan to put in his two cents' worth.

"O.K., boss, I'll take it."

With a smile, his father gave his blessing, which meant that Hans and Jan were not only good friends but also co-workers. From that time on, Jan observed the custom in that boilingly hot country of having an hour's siesta after lunch. But at the stroke of two, he jumped on the bicycle he had bought with his own hard-earned money and, at precisely half past two, reported for work with his new employer, Hans Nittel from Austria, now in Thailand as a hydraulic engineer for the World Health Organization.

Chapter Three

❖❖❖❖

A LETTER AND A CHASE AFTER THIEVES

Mrs. Grundvahl and Jan had eaten lunch, after which each went to his own darkened room to rest for a while. Jan threw himself onto his bed but found it impossible to sleep. He decided instead to write a long letter to his friend and classmate, Karl-Axel Alexandersson, back home in Sweden.

Dear Karlax:

Well, to begin with, maybe I'd better tell you how we're living here in Bangkok. The house is right in the middle of a huge garden, which is spilling over with every imaginable kind of flower, bush, and tree, not one of which looks like any vegetation at home. Imagine, if you can, that we have five gigantic palms in the garden—there are more palms here than any other kind of tree—and sometimes there are small monkeys playing among the huge leaves in the treetops. This can be pretty amusing to watch, but if you get too close, they stink like I don't know what.

The house itself doesn't have a cellar or any regular foundations, since it stands on a number of solid poles. According to what I've heard, the Thailanders always put their

houses on these stilts so that snakes and other kindred animals can't creep in. Here in the city there are no snakes—at
least I hope there aren't—but out in the country there are
loads of them that are so poisonous that thousands of people die of snake bite every year. The poles that support the
house are necessary for another reason—if they weren't
there, the water could wash the house away some fine day.
During the rainy season, a huge black cloud will suddenly
rise up and turn the day into almost pitch-black darkness,
after which it begins to rain—and you have no idea what a
downpour this is! It's not so much like a rainstorm as it is a
cascading waterfall. Fortunately, it doesn't last more than
an hour at the most, after which the sun comes out and the
sky is blue again. This goes on day after day after day for the
whole rainy season, one or two times a day, and after each
rainfall there are puddles as big as lakes everywhere,
including the main streets of the city.

Our house is pretty large. We have six rooms, none
of which has much furniture in it, and each room has windows almost wall to wall. Clear around the house is an open
veranda, over which we have raffia awnings as a protection
against the sun. If we didn't have these huge windows and
awnings, we'd never make it in this heat. At the moment it
isn't terribly hot, but my father has promised that I will
have the joy of experiencing 110° or 120° from February to
May—the summer season here. Joy? Well, we'll see.

The house we live in is built of heavy bamboo poles, the
commonest construction material here. Bangkok is a big
city, of course, and there are a number of modern concrete
buildings, which would be just as much at home in Sweden

as here, but concrete buildings are the exception rather than the rule here at the moment.

Mama has hired a cook and a servant. I'm sure you'll go tell everyone that we've become millionaires, but that isn't the case at all. It's just the way things are here—all the Caucasian families, and not only those but also the Thailand families who are well off, have servants. For that matter, Mama says that we simply couldn't get along without a cook here. In the beginning she tried to keep house all by herself, just as she does at home, but little by little she discovered that she had to pay at least twice as much for the food she bought in the market. "Farangs," the name the Thailanders use for Caucasians, always have to pay more than the native shoppers do.

The Chinese cook's name is Chan, and he's great with food. Mama has taught him to fix a few Swedish dishes, too, but mainly we eat Thailand or Chinese food. Mostly this consists of rice with bits of meat or fish mixed in with fruit and seasoned with spices I don't even know the names of. This sort of food is much better suited to the climate than brown beans and pork and stuff like that.

As you know, I'm nuts about fruit, so this country is heaven on earth as far as I'm concerned. There are thousands of kinds of fruit here, and they cost almost nothing. Take bananas, for instance. There are at least twenty different kinds, and each one tastes unique. In addition, I stuff myself with papaws, mangoes, a kind of watermelon, fresh figs, avocado, and a whole lot of others whose names I don't even know.

Chan speaks English, though his accent would kill you sometimes. I've gone with him to the open-air market, and that was quite a deal, let me tell you. The place swarms with guys in knee-length pants and shirts and women in long skirts, all of whom haggle and bargain with the farmers who bring their products in from the country. Most of the women who run the stands are elderly farm women with closely cropped hair. Some of them are actually baldies. Chan tells me that the old ladies who have their heads shaved are widows, and that they shave their heads to show that they have withdrawn from the futility of the world. Well, that's what he says, anyway.

I think the most fun of all is the fishmarket, where there are hundreds of different kinds of fish and lots of worms. Believe it or not, the Thailanders make a sort of paté out of these different kinds of worms, and they even insist that it's edible. Don't ask me, because I've never tasted any of it, and I am not about to unless someone forces me.

So far I've been gabbing about food and such, but I haven't said a word about the city itself. Well, here you have Bangkok. The city is situated at the mouth of a river that is very broad and as filthy as anything you've ever seen. On our side of the river is the royal palace with its red and green roof, and there are some Buddhist temples with gilded towers, but apart from these our side isn't particularly interesting. But you should see the other side! There the people have dug the most marvelous network of canals dating back hundreds of years, which means that the river has branches growing out of its branches. Along these canals and offshoots lives half the population of Bangkok, in huts that stand on poles out in the water or in houses built on barges. A number of them simply live in boats anchored along the banks. In addition to the houses on these canal streets, there are shops, work-

shops, and even movie houses, although there are no sidewalks or roads—just canals. The bamboo houses are built
so closely together that if you want to go and see a neighbor,
you can do so in a hop, skip, and jump.

You can see why this is called the Venice of Asia. People
paddle around in small boats whenever they want to go any
place, or else they just swim to where they work. The traffic
on the water is always fantastic, with barges and motorboats
bumping one another, children ducking, playing, and
splashing around in the water, and women washing their
clothes. In the bigger canals there are large boats that deliver goods to the shops. On market days the boats of the
sellers are packed in so tightly that you can scarcely see the
water, and all of them are loaded with fruit, vegetables, and
flowers. You probably know that the Thailanders love
flowers . . ."

Jan had gotten to this point in his letter when he happened
to look at the clock. Five after two! He had just pushed aside
his paper and pen and was putting on his light-weight tennis
shoes (which almost all Europeans wear in Bangkok) when
he noticed that it was suddenly getting very dark outside.
Jan knew what this meant—the usual daily rainstorm. The
sheets of rain were so heavy that you couldn't see more than
ten feet ahead of you, and all drivers simply had to come to
a stop until the downpour was over. At the same time, the
wind began to blow fiercely, and the trunks of the tall palms
in the garden were bent down almost to the ground. Real
Judgment Day weather, Jan had thought in his fright at seeing a rain of that sort for the first time.

Today the Thai rain goddess' wrist watch is way off, Jan

thought to himself, because this time she had opened the flood gates a half hour earlier than usual. Generally he had already arrived at work by the time the rain began, and they would spend the half hour while it poured in a quiet game of chess. Once the rain had ceased and the game was over, they would get to work again with renewed energy. But at the moment, all Jan could do was stand there drumming his fingers impatiently on the windowsill. It annoyed him to miss the game because the previous evening he had found a queen gambit in a chess handbook that he was dying to try out on Hans.

At last the downpour was over, just as suddenly as it had begun. Jan said good-by to his mother—his father hadn't come home to lunch that day—and walked his bicycle out to the street through the lush green garden. The road was

still soaked from the rain, which meant that it took him thirty-two minutes to get to work instead of the usual twenty-seven.

The place where he worked was a rather large area that
Hans had had fenced in with barbed wire. A part of the area
was allocated to warehouses for the long iron pipes, and each
time a new shipment arrived at the harbor, things were busy
in the warehouses. The delivery trucks came and went, and
small muscular Thailanders unloaded the pipes noisily,
while Hans, with the customs papers in hand, checked to see
that nothing was missing.

In another part of the area were some sheds of rush mat-
ting, bamboo poles, and raffia, surrounded by moats, which
were for storing the heavy paper sacks of cement to be used
for the digging frame and superstructure. And on the very
edge of the property, facing the entrance, was the place in
which Hans had his office and living quarters—an old mil-
itary barrack building that was now being put to the peaceful
purposes of well-digging.

As usual, Hans stood at the big drawing board inside the
office, ruling red and blue lines on a map—not an easy map
for the uninitiated to understand. It was no ordinary surface
map but a geological one, showing the different ground
strata and their respective thicknesses. With Hans's help
Jan had begun to be able to read these maps, but he was far
from an expert on the subject. Still, he knew enough to be
able to help with the work, even if his duties consisted mainly
of keeping the maps in order, rolling them up after their use,
and putting them back in the aluminum foil. To be sure,
he had other duties, too. Hans had taught him to use the
photocopy enlarger in the corner of the room, with which
he made copies of different sections of the larger maps as
Hans directed him.

Jan needed only to glance at Hans this afternoon to realize that something unpleasant must have taken place.

"Is something wrong?" Jan asked.

"Wrong? Well, not exactly. I just didn't get much sleep last night. It's not good for my disposition to compete in boat races at midnight."

"What are you talking about?" Jan asked in surprise. "Racing boats at midnight? Is this some strange habit of the Thailanders?"

"It would seem so. And poor old Pramodya, the night watchman, got hit on the head and had to be taken to the hospital."

"Oh, no!" Jan cried. "I don't understand what you're talking about. I think you'd better start at the beginning and tell me who knocked out Pramodya and why you were in a boat race in the middle of the night."

Hans pushed aside the map he was working on, took two Coca-Colas out of the refrigerator, and sat down.

"Yesterday evening I drove the jeep into the city to get my supper," he began. "I went to that Hungarian restaurant where we were with your parents recently—the one that has such good goulash. Afterwards I had a cup of coffee in a terrace café and talked with some acquaintances there. I was pretty tired, which is why I went home about ten or so. As soon as I got here, I knew something must have happened because the gate was wide open. And I remembered very well that old Pramodya had locked it after me because I heard the squeak of the lock when he shut it.

"I went straight over to the barrack, and when I got there, I almost fell over the old man who lay unconscious at the door. I hopped out of the jeep and lifted him in. He had a huge gash on his bald pate, and blood was oozing out. His clothes were covered with blood, and I realized that someone must have hit him on the head from the rear with a blunt object. While I was trying to bring him back to life, I suddenly heard sounds from inside the building. As you know, I always have a revolver with me, although I carry it more as a protection from animals than from people. Out here, with the jungle so close to us, it could easily happen that some wild animal might wander into the area. I took the revolver out of my back pocket and started to go into the barrack, but the door was locked from the inside, and I couldn't get it open. Then I walked over to one of the windows, and through the insect netting I could see two figures taking the aluminum-foil bundles out of the map cabinet."

"Hey, just a minute," Jan interrupted. "What time do you usually come home after supper?"

"Well, that's hard to say. Different times. In this heat you can't sleep, and sometimes I hang around one or another of the outside cafés enjoying the cool of the evening. The evenings when I eat at the tennis club, I usually play bridge afterwards. Most of the time I don't get back home before eleven or so. Why?"

"Well, the thieves could have known all about your habits and not counted on being caught in the act."

"True. I haven't eliminated that possibility, even though I can't figure out how they could establish the time when I usually get home. There are no buildings in the vicinity, and no other people live around here."

"Well, they could have questioned old Pramodya and

made him tell all about the life of debauchery his boss lives."

"Thanks a lot!" Hans laughed. "Not badly put—my life of debauchery. But the old man would never have had a chance to betray the dark secrets of my life to any un-authorized person. He can't tell time, and he's usually asleep long before I get back home. But to get back to the story. That isn't the end. It's just the beginning. When I discovered what the two guys were up to, I pointed my revolver at them and threatened them with 'Hands up or I'll shoot.' Unfortunately, they paid no attention. They didn't raise their arms but instead disappeared in a twinkling into my bed-room. Before I had time to circle around to the bedroom window, they had returned to the office. So we went on playing hide and seek until I got tired of it. I hurried over to the entrance and shot the lock apart. But when I got the door open, with the revolver butt ready to strike, and went into the office, nobody was there."

"That's not so strange," Jan said. "They weren't foolish enough to hang around waiting for you when all they had to do was go out a window."

"Right you are. I can tell you read detective stories because that's exactly what they did. But I didn't give up. I chased after them. They had at least a hundred yards' lead over me, and as you know, Thailanders are fine runners. I can run four hundred meters in 54.55 approximately, but no matter how fast I went, I couldn't catch up with the thieves. No doubt I would have given up the chase early in the game if they hadn't headed down toward the riverbank. There I figured I could get them."

"And why were you so certain that you could get them there?" Jan asked.

"I forgot to tell you that each one had taken a roll of maps. You know how hard maps are to come by around here, and those had been drawn to order and are almost irreplaceable, so naturally I was desperate to get them back. If they had just dropped the bundles, I wouldn't have given a thought to following them."

"Well, did you get the maps back?"

"No, I didn't. But let me tell you everything in the order in which it happened. When the two thieves got down to the shore, they piled into a little boat that was tied up ten or twenty yards from my own motorboat. Before I could untie my boat and get it started, they were already a good distance out on the river. Still I felt I had the better of them this time, but to my great astonishment, it turned out that their boat was motorized, too. Apparently they hadn't been able to get it going right away, because to begin with, I didn't hear any motor noise. Because of this I managed to close in so that I was only about fifty yards from them when they swerved off into a narrow canal. I was pretty nervous about following them around in the dark, but I kept on. They must really have been at home in the area, judging by the way they darted in and out among the tiny water alleys. The sputtering motor, of course, always indicated approximately where they were, so I could go on with the chase."

"Tell me, why didn't you shoot at some point?" Jan asked.

"Well, in the first place, you don't have any right to shoot down anyone, even a thief, just willy-nilly, and in the second place, the odds weren't great that I could hit them at a distance of fifty or sixty yards in pitch darkness. So we continued to play cops and robbers for a while. Some of the inhabitants of the boats and barges were awakened by the sounds of the motors, and their comments on our wild chase weren't exactly flattering. But gradually, the thieves began to tire of the game. Suddenly the putt-putt of their motor died down after they had turned off into a new canal. At first I was overjoyed, thinking that they had run out of gas. I watched them steering the boat in toward a stair landing below a house, where they jumped out and headed up the steps. Naturally, I followed their example—steered my boat to the same stair landing and rushed into the house. But that I should never have done!"

"Weren't they there?"

"Not at all. The only person in the vicinity of the bamboo hut was an older man with a thin white beard—a real goatee. But I didn't see hide nor hair of the thieves. And it was a hopeless matter asking the old man any questions, because he merely stared wide-eyed at me, mumbling, '*Om mani padme hum, om mani padme hum,*' at the speed of about a hundred twenty times a minute."

"What in the world is that?"

"It's Tibetan, and literally translated, it means something like, 'Oh you gem in the lotus blossom.' I think its real meaning is something like, 'God have mercy on my soul.' It turned out that the old man was Tibetan and didn't understand a word of any language other than Tibetan. And while I was searching the various rooms and poking around in the outer corridor, I suddenly heard the noise of the motor again. Well, the two thieves had sneaked out some side door or window, gotten into my boat, tied their own on behind, started the motor, and buzzed out into the canal again. Before I got down there, they were far away and were swallowed up in the darkness almost at once. And with them my motorboat!"

"How did you get home?"

"It took quite a while for me to awaken a guy in one of the neighboring houses, who, for a reasonable fee, took me over to the other bank. It was past midnight before I got back home after the unsuccessful chase. On the way home, I suddenly realized that in the excitement of the chase I had completely forgotten about old Pramodya who lay there unconscious. Naturally, I should have driven him to the nearest hospital first, instead of running like an idiot after the thieves. Even at that, it wasn't too bad. I found the old man in his own little den. He had come to while I was away and had even dressed his wound as well as he could, but he still seemed pretty befuddled to me. So I put him in the jeep and drove him to the municipal hospital, where the doctor assured me that his injuries weren't very serious. Still, he had suffered a slight brain concussion, and just to be on the safe side, they decided to keep him in the hospital until he's fully recovered."

"Did you tell all this to the police?"

"Of course. I was there the whole morning. What it has taken me ten minutes to tell you took three hours to pound into the thick heads of the police. The officials down there had a million questions on every imaginable detail, and they took down everything I answered. I'm very curious to know whether or not they will ever be able to catch the thieves, because first they filled up ten pages of notes as to where I had gone to school, when I was last vaccinated against smallpox, and how much I weigh stripped."

"That's a little unfair," Jan said with a laugh. "It's not so strange that the police wanted to go over every detail. Possibly some small, insignificant matter can set them on the right track."

"There you go with your detective stories again. Well, we'll just have to wait and see what the Sherlock Holmeses of Thailand can come up with. They managed to find out that I didn't have a Thailand license for weapons, and I didn't help matters a bit by waving my Austrian license in front of their noses. They made me pay a fine of ten *ticals!*"

"Well, at least you got something out of your visit to the police station."

"Anyway, I have now checked," Hans continued, growing serious again, "and know that the thieves took with them the maps for wells numbered four and seven. I haven't been able to figure out why they were interested in those two particularly. One well is to be drilled on the outskirts of one of the suburbs to the north, and the other on the opposite side of the river. These spots are quite a distance from each other. Of course, it might just be a coincidence that they took the two they did."

Jan sat deep in contemplation as he listened to his friend's account. As for himself, he had thought of another explanation.

"Are you absolutely sure that the maps were what the thieves were after, Hans? Isn't it possible that they didn't have any idea what the maps were all about and simply wanted to steal something of worth? When they caught sight of the aluminum-foil rolls, perhaps they thought the contents were something expensive or precious and just took them? As I see it, that sounds pretty logical?"

"You might just be right. Anyway, I went straight to a

locksmith when I left the police headquarters, and he has now installed a new lock on the barrack door. We need a new watchman, too, for I'm pretty sure that old Pramodya won't be back right away. For that matter, I'm far from certain he'll want to continue in a job as dangerous as this one. The end result is that we'll have to try getting new copies of the missing maps from the Geological Institute at Chulalongkorn University. And that can take a great deal of time."

Chapter Four

❖❖❖❖

SNIT ENTERS THE PICTURE

Not much work was accomplished that afternoon. First three carloads of policemen came out to the establishment to inspect the scene of the crime. Naturally, Hans and Jan took part in it all, with the engineer reiterating the events of the previous night three times in a row, pointing out where he had found the old night watchman, telling them through which window he had first caught sight of the thieves, and demonstrating for them how he had shot the lock apart and where the maps had been kept.

Hardly had the police finished their inspection when visitors began to arrive. A little distance to the south of the construction site was a district overflowing with bamboo huts— one of Bangkok's countless suburbs, which stretched clear down to the banks of the river, where a Buddhist temple with a cloister alongside lifted its gilded spires toward the sky.

Hans was very popular with the people of the district, not the least reason for which was the fact that he was eagerly learning the Thai language and never lost an opportunity to improve his conversational ability. *Farang* engineer, as he

was called in the district, was soon a popular conversation-
alist.

One afternoon Hans had invited the inhabitants of the
nearby houses to take a look at the construction site and had
passed around tea and small rice cookies. Afterwards, he had
made a little speech in which he told them that the huge
river, without doubt, was a blessing and a sign of prosperity
to the Thailanders. The waters of the river, of course, running through the canals and out onto the rice fields, made
possible the rice they lived on. The river was also a means
of communication and, as such, had great meaning. He went
on to explain that the water, however, was not suitable for
drinking.

Hans explained that he had come to draw up cold, crystal-
clear water from the interior of the earth, to drill artesian
wells that would supply everyone with fresh, healthful
drinking water at no cost to them. The Thailanders are not
only clean by nature but are also highly intelligent. That
they had used the river waters for so many purposes merely
meant that they had had no other choice. Hans's little lecture
had been received with understanding and approval. When
he later showed them the whole construction site, the sacks
of cement, the pipes, and the special geological maps, they
had taken him to their hearts together with the entire project.

Gradually, he discovered another way to win the sympathy
of the surrounding people. He found out that three young
monks from the cloister made their rounds of the village
every single morning. Each one held in his outstretched
hands a large copper kettle. The women stood outside their
houses waiting for them to arrive, and as the monks

approached, each one deposited a portion of cooked rice in the monk's kettle. Never did the monks thank them for their gifts but continued on, with downcast eyes, to the next house, where the ceremony was repeated.

These strange rites originated because the monks, according to the rules of the cloister, were not allowed to work or to handle money. Neither could they beg, but the faithful regarded it as their solemn duty to provide for their subsistence. The food collected in the huge copper kettles was returned by them to the cloister, where, at mealtime, it was shared by all the monks. This was their only meal of the day. Apart from this repast and a short recess thereafter, the monks with their saffron-yellow robes and their shaven heads spent all their time studying the Holy Scriptures. Since the Thailanders are Buddhists, they hold monks in high esteem, and most of the men in the country voluntarily spend several months of their lives as monks, subject to the strict way of life of the cloister.

Hans knew all about this and soon, therefore, instructed old Pramodya to go off every morning to the outskirts of the village, wait for the monks with the copper kettles, and put a bowl of rice and vegetables in the nearest kettle. Pramodya himself was a devout Buddhist who more than willingly accepted the assignment.

No one knew whether the tea party, the informational lecture, or the daily pious gift was responsible, but whatever it was, one day Hans received an invitation to visit the abbot of the cloister. Before going there, Pramodya had told him that it was the custom on such occasions to take some flowers, kneel before one of the cloister's countless statues of Buddha, and place the flowers there as an offering, after which one

would clap three times in order to call the god's attention to
the gift. That it was blasphemous and disrespectful to enter
the confines of the cloister wearing shoes Hans already knew.

His visit was successful in every respect. The abbot, it
turned out, was a well-educated, distinguished elderly man
who spoke perfect English. He felt a certain respect for Hans
who, during the conversation, defended his Christian beliefs
but who, at the same time, spoke with the highest esteem of
the great religious leader, Buddha. The people of the district
were devoted to the learned abbot, and when the news got
around that the *farang* engineer had spent a whole hour
with the abbot, Hans's stock among the local people climbed
several points.

On the afternoon after the theft, the neighbors from the
nearby suburb streamed in to express their regrets over the
events of the previous night. The visitors bowed three times
with their hands crossed over their chests, and Hans and Jan
returned their greetings in the same fashion. Each and every
one of the callers emphasized his own deep personal shame
over what had happened, condemned the thieves with all
his heart, and assured them that they were not from the
district but were doubtless strangers. After their short dis-
courses, each one gave Hans, more or less as a peace offering,
a small bouquet of flowers. Gradually, the office began to
look like a huge garden.

Suddenly, there was much hustle and bustle among those
who were waiting outside the barrack. Jan went to find out
what was going on. Three men in yellow robes were approaching the establishment.

Hans, too, went outside and began to whisper to the astonished Jan, "That's the abbot himself with two of his monks!"

Hans hurried to the main entrance to receive his honored guests, and everyone standing outside the barrack bowed deeply until the abbot and both of his disciples had entered Hans's office. The abbot said about the same things as the other visitors had, but in English rather than Thai. Hans bowed three times and thanked him for the great honor of his visit, simultaneously assuring the abbot that the crime wasn't going to cause him to come to any wrong conclusions about the neighboring people and the consequent delay in his work.

"I thank you for those kind statements, my son. I know that you, like all righteous people, are fond of my people, and I beg you in the future to continue holding us in affection," the elderly man said as he prepared to depart.

Dusk was falling, and Jan had to go home for dinner. Slowly, the visitors began wending their way home also, leaving Hans alone at the plant. After what had happened, he didn't want to leave the area unguarded, so he heated up some canned food instead of riding into the city to eat.

The following day when Jan came out to the construction site, Hans told him that during the morning he had called on old Pramodya at the hospital, that he had ordered new maps from the geological institute, and that the factory in Europe from which he had ordered the drill and other heavy equipment had informed him that the full order had been shipped on the M.S. Sutherland.

Since there was nothing particular to be done at the moment, Jan suggested a game of ping-pong. It hadn't taken him long to discover that the big drawing board could be converted into a fine tennis table once they moved it out into the open. He had also bought two paddles, a net, and a dozen balls with money that his father had given him on the condition that he, too, might be allowed to play now and then.

The table-tennis equipment, received with great ceremony, had had its premiere on a Sunday afternoon with Mrs. Grundvahl making it a foursome. Among the three masculine contenders, Hans won easily. Finally he revealed that some years back he had been the table-tennis champion of Innsbruck, so his victory was not coincidence. Neither Jan nor his father could offer much real competition for his curving serves and forehand drives.

But Hans was so absorbed in his work that very seldom would he let himself be talked into quitting a little early and taking time for a ping-pong game.

After a while, a new and less busy ping-pong partner for Jan entered the picture. One afternoon, just when he had managed to talk Hans into a game, a young Thailander wandered into the area. He was a heavy-set, strong, broad-shouldered boy, whose brown, symmetrical face radiated intelligence. He wore blue shorts and a clean sleeveless shirt. Politely bowing, the boy walked up to Hans, raised his clasped hands to his forehead, and handed a piece of paper to the engineer.

"The undersigned, Snit Labanukors, thirteen-year-old errand boy, begs herewith respectfully that the esteemed, honorable engineer *farang* allow this humble person to take part in the table-tennis game."

Later on, Snit told them that the note in English had been dictated to and written by one of the official letter writers who charged a fee of one *tical*. There were many such scribes in Bangkok. On almost every corner a scribe sat on a raffia mat behind a small, low board, and for a small fee he would compose eloquent letters or official documents, in accordance with the wishes of the customer, in Thai, Chinese, Hindu, or even English.

Hans studied Snit's document seriously. It amused him
very much, actually, but he didn't dare laugh for fear of
hurting the feelings of the boy who stood there waiting for
an answer. Instead, he introduced himself with true Thai
courtesy by lifting his hand to his forehead, bowing to Snit
Labanukors, and saying to him in Thai, "I am very honored
by Mr. Labanukors' request. Naturally, he is welcome to
take part in our humble enjoyment."

His great joy—or perhaps surprise at hearing the *farang*
speaking Thai—caused Snit to grow pale; he almost forgot
to say thank you. Hans shoved a racket into his hand and
invited him immediately to challenge Jan to a game. After
Snit and Jan had introduced themselves, bowing eagerly, the
game began. It was obvious from the beginning that Snit had
never played table tennis before, and he missed the small
ball more often than he hit it. After playing for half an hour
—a period that was rather tedious for Jan—Snit began to
catch on, and it was soon evident that he would be a fine
player with a little more practice.

Once the game was over, Snit told them that he lived in
a bamboo house on a float in the river. He had not been born
in Bangkok but had come from a little village in the mountainous southeastern part of the country. A couple of years
back his parents had died in an epidemic, at which point
Snit's oldest brother had inherited their little rice field. Soon
thereafter, the brother had given Snit fifty *ticals* and sent
him out into the world. Such a small piece of ground couldn't
support the family or keep all its members busy.

Snit had gone by foot to the huge river. There he had taken
a job on a rice freighter, which was how he had come to
Bangkok. For five months he had been working as an errand

boy in a food store in the canal district. Early in the morning, when the farmers from the small villages around the capital arrived with their wares, Snit and his employer would row out to their boats, where Snit would help with the buying. Later, also by boat, he delivered orders to customers, helped in the warehouse, and kept the shop clean. His salary wasn't much, but since he received food from his employer—that is, he ate with him and his family—and since he paid no more than two *ticals* a week for his room on the float, he was actually quite happy with his lot. The only thing was that it was a little hard to find things to do in his free time. He had been to the movies occasionally, which he had enjoyed very much, but this was very expensive. For this reason, he had used some of his spare time in rowing across the river, standing by the construction site fence, and staring at what was going on inside. On one such occasion, he had seen Hans and Jan playing ping-pong, and the sight had awakened such a burning desire in him to play that he had sacrificed a whole *tical* to have his wish committed to paper. Had he known earlier that Hans could speak Thai, he could have saved his money and gone to the movies. But it was too late to think about that now . . .

Both Hans and Jan were fond of Snit from the beginning, and they gave him, once and for all, permission to call on them whenever he was free from his job. The boy made good use of this privilege, popping up one or two times a week, usually during the afternoon when the shop where he worked was closed.

Very quickly, he and Jan became fast friends, and within no time at all they could converse with one another in a great hodgepodge of language. Jan began to teach Snit some English, and he, in turn, began to initiate Jan into some of the mysteries of Thai. They were not long in discovering that Snit had an easier time learning languages than did Jan.

Table tennis came to him even more easily than English. The fourth time they met, Jan had to work pretty hard in order to remain undefeated. By pure instinct, Snit held the racket the same as the Chinese world's champions did. His eyes were sharp, he was good with the ball, and there was an unbelievable amount of agility in his spindly brown legs. In addition, he threw his whole body into the game, as if his entire future depended upon the ping-pong ball.

On this particular afternoon, Snit appeared while Jan and Hans were moving the drawing board out in the yard. "He seems to have a sixth sense that tells him when we have a game in mind," Jan mused to himself. But this time Snit had not come to play ping-pong; he was here on a much more important mission. It was evident at once that something unusual had taken place, because he wasn't like his usual self. His generally calm, smiling face was pained and worried. His clothes were not as clean as usual, especially the white shirt. Wrinkled and soiled, it needed a good washing. He even forgot his customary greeting and his three bows as he turned to Hans nervously, almost shouting, "You've got to come with me at once, Engineer. Now. Right away . . ."

"What's the matter with you, Snit? You look as if you've taken leave of your senses." Hans said in surprise.

"Don't stop to ask questions. Just come along," Snit replied in a pleading tone of voice.

Hans and Jan realized that Snit was obviously not receptive to questions at the moment, so without a word they followed the boy down to the shore. Snit ran more than walked, and they had a hard time keeping up with him. Finally, they made their way down to the river, right at the place where Hans's motorboat had formerly been tied to a small pier. And, strangely enough, there it was again, bobbing up and down on the waves, as if the thieves had never laid hands on it.

Hans gave a cry of surprise and ran over to the boat. The craft was important to his work because, without it, he had difficulty in getting to the digging locations along the river.

"Well, how did that get back here?" he asked Snit.

"I'm the one who brought it here," the boy replied proudly. "When I heard that it had been stolen, I asked my employer for some time off and borrowed a small boat from one of my neighbors. Then I paddled around all day long until it was dark, and as soon as it was daylight again, I continued to search through the canals in an effort to track down your motorboat. I had already combed all the big main canals and had gone through a good many of the side branches, too, when this afternoon I found it in a narrow water alley. It was tied up to a pier, together with two other boats. I asked everyone in the neighborhood, but no one knew how it had gotten there or who the owner was. At least that's what they all said. And now you have it back. I don't want you to think that we Thailanders are all thieves."

"I certainly never had such a thought," Hans answered. "But after all those hours of paddling around, you must be pretty tired. And since you haven't been working, I'm sure you haven't eaten either. Come along now and I'll drive you home, and we can get a bite to eat at one of the shore restaurants along the way."

Without a protest, Snit got into the motorboat. Hans checked and found that the thieves had actually left a little gas in the tank, enough to get them over to the nearest gas station along the shore. They tied Snit's boat behind and started the motor.

Hans directed the boat diagonally across the river toward a building on poles out in the water. There was a restaurant in the building, where they all squatted down on raffia mats at a small low table and ordered a bowl each of heavily spiced rice mixed with fish, which they washed down with lemon soda. Snit must have been starved because he wolfed down his food.

When they had dropped Snit at the float where he lived, Hans looked at his watch.

"Five," he exclaimed. "I hope there's someone left at the police station."

"What are you going to do there?" Jan asked.

"I have to let them know, of course, that we've gotten the motorboat back. Just imagine a whole gang of policemen spending all their time going over Bangkok with a fine-tooth comb, searching for my boat!"

Going across to the other side again, they walked up to the construction site and got in the jeep. Jan couldn't resist the temptation to go with Hans to the police station. He was curious to know what the police looked like and how they operated in Thailand. This gave him the opportunity to confirm a secret suspicion—that the police were just as fond of elegant clothing as were most Thailanders. On all holidays and feast days—and there are many of these in Thailand— the Thailanders all dress up in their national costumes. The women parade in their bright red, yellow, and green garments, their long, narrow sarongs of beautiful silk, and their sleeveless blouses, while the men wear elegant headdresses and broad silk sashes. As the procession passes through Bangkok on a holiday, the city looks like a Hollywood technicolor director's dream.

The police officer had neither a variegated headdress nor a wide sash with red and yellow stripes, but his elegant uniform would have been a match for any American officer. The designer of the uniform had not been stingy with gilt, which appeared almost everywhere from the buttons all the way to the wide shoulder straps and the cordon across his chest. The man received Hans with great friendliness, but his face clouded up as he found out that the motorboat was back in the hands of its owner.

"Actually, the boy, who was unauthorized, has interfered in the work of the police," he explained, "and this sort of procedure is definitely not condoned."

"I understand your point of view," Hans answered, "but you can certainly look upon these as extenuating circumstances. And the boy really did find the motorboat. I hope that the honored policeman will take that matter into account."

As soon as they left the police station, the astonished Jan asked Hans for elucidation of this totally unfathomable exchange of words.

"I can imagine that you didn't understand, because you haven't had anything to do with the Thailand authorities up to now. As for myself, I have had a good bit of experience with them, especially when I first came and was occupied with staking out the digging locations. The public servants here are always amiable and also quite helpful, in their own fashion. But if you butt into any of their concerns, they are immediately insulted, at which point they can be as stubborn as mules. I am delighted that I was able to keep the police from arresting Snit," Hans explained, to Jan's astonishment.

Though Snit was not arrested, that same evening he was taken to the station by one of the policemen and questioned half the night in an attempt to find out how he had been successful in finding Hans's motorboat. The next morning one of the police motorboats came to take him to the place where he'd discovered it. In the afternoon he was once more at the police station telling the police over and over the whole chain of events. After that there was more questioning about the boat and much additional protocol among the police.

Finally, on the third day, when Snit, completely worn out and red-eyed with sleeplessness, reported back to his job, the employer explained that he had already hired a replacement for him. "I couldn't keep my customers waiting until you cleared up all those matters with the police," he said. "For that matter, I really don't like to have anyone in my employ who has had anything to do with the police."

That day Hans and Jan waited for Snit in vain. The next morning Hans took his motorboat and went to the float where the boy lived. Luckily, he found the boy at home. He was bathing in the river and vigorously brushing his teeth. However, it took a lot of patient questioning and persuasion before Snit finally revealed that he had lost his job.

"Don't worry about that, Snit," Hans said immediately. "I've been wondering a good deal how I could thank you for getting my motorboat back. Now I don't have to concern myself any longer. Our former night watchman has told me that he doesn't want to work with us again after he gets out of the hospital. He is afraid of the job. So, if you wish, you can take over as watchman, effective at once."

Snit's face broke out in a Cheshire cat grin, but soon his countenance clouded.

"Well, you see, I will have to tell you a secret, Engineer. I have a dog. He lives here with me on the float, and he usually tags along with me when I deliver orders. He's a very ordinary dog and not very good-looking exactly, but he came with me from my home country, and I have no desire to abandon a countryman here in the middle of a big city—on the loose . . ."

Hans laughed, but at the same time he was very moved. He himself was very fond of dogs but had been compelled to leave his own pet at home in Innsbruck.

"It doesn't matter to me if you have a dog, Snit. Just bring him along with you. I'm sure we can find a corner for him, and he'll be a help as a watchdog. What is your dog's name, anyway?"

Snit looked at him, a bit puzzled.

"He isn't a good enough dog to have a name of his own. I just call him 'dog.' Or else I whistle at him."

He demonstrated the latter by letting out a shrill whistle. Immediately, a loud bark was heard, accompanied by violent splashing from the shore, and a few seconds later a soaking-wet dog stood on the float shaking the water off itself.

Snit's countryman was no beauty; the boy was right about that. He was ocher yellow and had a long, narrow tail that swung upward in the shape of a question mark. His nose and ears were black. And the poor creature was so skinny that you could count every single rib. But when Snit lifted him into the motorboat and sat down with the mongrel beside him, he showed the animal the kind of tenderness that you would show a dog that had won first prize at the kennel show.

Chapter Five

❖❖❖❖

A SHIP COMES LOADED

"Finally!" Hans sighed as he sat with Bangkok's English-language newspaper in hand. For a couple of weeks, he had studied the newspaper daily with more interest than usual, and each time he had directed his attention first to the last page, where there was a special column on ship arrivals and departures. The day finally came when he saw the notice of the ship he was so eagerly awaiting, the *M.S. Sutherland,* which had in its hold the equipment he was going to need for the digging.

"Finally!" he said to his table companions, Jan and his father. "All the calculations have been made and the preparations accomplished, so that we can now get down to digging —the real work."

"Not so fast." Mr. Grundvahl grinned. "You've got to count on the fact that it will be a good while before the boat gets to the dock, and more time while the goods are unloaded, sent through customs, and stored before they can be delivered out to the site. I think you'll have to be patient for a few days yet before you can begin."

"You're right about that, of course," Hans answered. "And

the master driller hasn't arrived yet, either. But in any case, we can hope that the authorities won't give us any great trouble. I'm sure the customs office will clear the shipment immediately. Everyone knows that we're working for the welfare of the people and that the digging of these wells is not costing the Thailand government a single cent. Up to this time, they have been favorably disposed to everything."

"Oh, absolutely," Mr. Grundvahl replied. "But you've got to keep in mind the fact that the mills of God grind slowly here in Asia, with a great deal of bureaucracy and red tape."

The next morning Hans, Jan, and Snit, the latter accompanied by Dog, stood out on the pier watching with great interest as the *Sutherland*, a dark green fifteen-thousand-ton British ship, maneuvered itself slowly and majestically into its berth at the pier. They were there in the afternoon, too, as the hoisting crane cautiously lifted up six voluminous wooden packing cases and lowered them to the platform outside the customs shed.

"Well, those are our cases," Hans said joyfully, adding, "I can take care of the customs tomorrow, but at least I can place my order with the delivery trucks today. If all goes well, we can have everything out at the site by tomorrow evening."

Hans was somewhat justified in his optimism, but not totally. The customs men were actually very obliging, and although they made Hans fill out a whole raft of forms and go through a great many formalities, they didn't present too many difficulties. Hans received permission to load the packing cases onto the two trucks that were parked and waiting outside. But . . .

When the packing cases were brought from the warehouse, it turned out that there were only five of them instead of six. All Hans's inquiries seemed to be in vain. There were only five cases from the factory supplying the well-digging concern. But Hans and Jan recalled very clearly that six cases had been unloaded from the *Sutherland*—not five. They could also state positively that the sixth case had been put ashore, a fact verified by the bill of lading that the captain of the *Sutherland* had delivered to customs.

But where had the sixth case gone? That question, for the next few days, was uppermost in not only the minds of Hans and Jan, but also the harbor captain, his employees, and all of the customs men. Everyone did his utmost to trace the missing case because, in the light of Hans's explanations, they had all seen at once what a blessing the wells with fresh, pure drinking water would be for the people of Bangkok.

Right from the start, they were able to eliminate the possibility that a common harbor thief could have gotten hold of the missing case. Since the cases contained all sorts of iron parts and weighed at least half a ton each, if not more, it would hardly have been possible for a thief, in broad daylight, to get away with anything so heavy and bulky right on the open pier. The harbor captain, however, ordered a general investigation and questioned every customs man and harbor worker personally in his office. On the third day, they got a small lead. One of the crane men and two stevedores were able to tell them that a man in a customs officer's uniform had come up to them the same day the cases had been unloaded and instructed them to return one of the cases to the hold of the ship. The three of them had no reason to believe that there was anything suspicious about his orders, whereupon they did as they had been told, returning the case to the hold of the *Sutherland*. The crane worker even recalled that the officer, before the packing case was hauled back, had been aboard the *Sutherland*, and upon his return to the pier, he had given them more detailed instructions as to how the case was to be hoisted back.

By the time they had learned this, the *Sutherland* was far away, already out on the open sea on the way to Rangoon, Burma. A couple of radio messages convinced the harbor captain that his men had been telling the truth. The packing case in question actually was in one of the *Sutherland*'s holds along with an assortment of piece goods. In his radio reply, the captain was even able to tell them that the case had been redirected to a well-known export firm in Rangoon.

Hans was understandably happy that the whereabouts of the machine parts had been established, but at the same time he was concerned over the fact that it might take weeks, even months, before the missent case could be shipped back to Bangkok. And this, in turn, would mean a dreadful delay with the start of the work at the digging sites. Having gotten this far, it was a shame that they couldn't get down to the real work of bringing up the crystal-clear water from the interior of the earth!

The harbor captain, not satisfied with merely knowing the whereabouts of the missing case, continued his investigation. Above all, he wanted to clear up the matter of who assumed the responsibility for getting the case back on the *Sutherland*. Once more he summoned the crane worker and the two stevedores to his office and had every uniformed harbor and customs man pass in review before them. However, not one of the three could identify the officer who had given them the orders to put the case back. Both of the stevedores remembered very clearly that the man in question had had a long, narrow scar, probably the aftermath of a knife wound, running the entire length of his left cheek. But none of the officers at the harbor had such a scar, and the harbor captain was sure that he had never had a person answering that description among his personnel.

Neither was there any record that the order to reload had been entered in the work register of the harbor. The whole thing seemed terribly suspicious, but acting on Hans's advice, the harbor captain kept the police from entering the mysterious case and taking over. Having learned from his experience with the robbery, Hans was averse to being dragged into the impenetrable jungle of protocol and questioning another time.

Meanwhile, out at the construction site, Hans, Jan, and Snit had unpacked the five cases. Hans was familiar with all the screw notches, boring tools, transformers, rings, and nails, but to both of the boys everything was new and exciting. They picked up every single part, turning it over and over in an attempt to guess what its purpose might be. Poor Hans was subjected to a stream of questions. After a while he didn't know which way to turn because of the bombardment of questions in English, Thai, and a sort of concocted mixture of languages.

The work and experiences they shared in common had made the friendship between Jan and Snit a very close one. Snit was making great progress in his language study, and soon Jan decided to initiate him into the mysteries of the Roman alphabet. Snit was not an illiterate; he was able to write the decorative symbols of Thai, and he could read both the Holy Scriptures of Buddha and the daily papers of Thailand. Actually, Jan was quite impressed with his learning, and he gained a certain respect for the instruction methods in the village schools of Thailand. He had read and heard so much about illiteracy in Africa and Asia, and even in parts of southern Europe, that he was aware of how much Snit's knowledge meant.

One afternoon as the boys were resting for a while in the shade of the barrack, Snit explained in his broken English how it had come about that he was so good at the art of writing.

"I'm sure you have heard," he began, "that we here in Thailand have an especially great respect for the people who consecrate their lives to their belief, who enter cloisters and spend their time studying our religion's Holy Scriptures. Buddhism teaches its disciples that the greatest virtue of all is the rejection of earthly temptations and the withdrawal from the sorrows and pleasures of everyday living. The model Buddhist is a person who loses himself totally in the reading of the Holy Scriptures so as to be able to contemplate and muse upon the riddles of the world.

"But naturally," he continued, "not everyone is suited to the life of the brotherhood in the cloister. The rules of the cloister, however, permit anyone to withdraw from the world temporarily and put on the saffron-yellow monk's robes. His head is shaved, and he must obey the rules of the cloister in all respects. If he tires of the isolation and the religious life, he is perfectly free to leave the cloister and return to his former life. There are many who do enter a cloister for several months, and people who are desirous of public esteem regard it as a duty to go back to a cloister every now and then to humble their bodies and intensify the realm of their souls.

"There are always several young boys in a cloister," Snit continued, "who are there more or less as pupils. They help keep things clean and neat, partake in the ceremonies, and are taught some of the more easily understood principles of the Scriptures by the elder brothers. As the boys get older, they can choose for themselves whether they want to be monks or return to the world. When I was ten years old, my parents sent me to the cloister just outside our village, and I spent two years there inside its walls. I learned a good bit, not only about our religion, but also about the art of concentration and independent thinking. I liked it there, and perhaps I would have stayed for good had I not been smitten with a terrible longing to see the world and learn to know faraway places."

"But do you think you'll ever go back and be a brother now that you've been in Bangkok for a while and seen other cities and villages on the way here?" Jan asked with interest.

"No, actually, I don't think I will," Snit replied. "Now that I've seen a little bit of the world, I'm beginning to understand how immense it is. Much more huge than I could have imagined when I lived at home in the village. Since coming here, I have been reading a lot about foreign countries; I've heard seamen telling about them, and I would love to travel and see other places, too."

"All of them? There are lots and lots of countries in the world, Snit!"

"I know, but I want to see all of them—every one of them. Your homeland, and the engineer's homeland, and Burma where the *Sutherland* is going, and England where the *Sutherland* came from. I want to see them all. And it would

make me very happy if you would tell me a little about your
country and its people."

Jan needed very little urging, and from that time on, he
would often, after a ping-pong match or writing practice
session, tell Snit about Sweden, his home town, and the
Swedish people, with special emphasis on the Swedish winter
with its snow and ice—something Snit had never experienced.

The days passed swiftly for Jan and Snit. Jan had two jobs
these days—he was Hans's co-worker, and he was Snit's
teacher. And he felt a great satisfaction at accomplishing
something useful and good in both respects.

A few days after the arrival of the drilling machinery, Hans
received a cablegram from the director of the World Health
Organization, telling him that they had been fortunate
enough to find a master driller, who would be arriving in
Bangkok by plane within a few days. George Grimes was
his name, and he was an American.

On the date mentioned in the cable, three or—if you were
to count Dog—three and a half people were out at the airport to meet Mr. Grimes. Jan had pictured him as a young,
broad-shouldered man with a crew cut, a broad smile, and
a striped cowboy shirt. The plane arrived on time, and the
passengers exited, but Jan, from his observation point on
the open terrace of the waiting room, couldn't see a single
soul that corresponded to his mental picture. Hans, on the
other hand, had no difficulty in identifying Mr. Grimes at
the passport control department on the lower floor. He
turned out to be the complete opposite of what Jan had imagined. In the first place, the American master driller was
in his forties and could not by any stretch of the imagination

be described as of more than medium height. Neither did he have a glistening, wide smile. To be truthful, he looked almost sullen. And in place of the cowboy shirt, he wore an elegant suit made of thin material, a spotless white shirt, and a dark blue necktie.

In spite of his sullen expression, Mr. Grimes seemed to be quite friendly. When Hans inquired, after all the formalities were over, where Mr. Grimes had in mind to live, he explained that he had already booked a room in one of the better hotels. This was a further disappointment to Jan, who had counted on his living at the site and becoming a welcome addition to the small circle of friends out there.

Leaving the airport, they went to the hotel in Hans's jeep. It would be more truthful to say that they crawled along, because the streets were thronged with people in their holiday costumes. It was a Buddhist holiday, and every reasonably vertical human being was out on the streets. The multitudes of yellow, red, and bright green garments almost blinded the eye in the brilliant sunshine. The display of colors was further enhanced by banners in every color of the rainbow, carried on long light bamboo poles held high above the heads of the crowd. It was as if both the people and the banners were swaying in the same rippling rhythm as the parade progressed through the streets. You could hardly see the sky for the fantastic silk, paper, and bamboo dragons afloat—a Chinese custom that the Thailanders had adopted as their own. The school children were not to be outdone by their masters, if one were to judge by the hundreds of flying kites in the form of terrible thorny black-and-yellow dragons, blue and red fish with wide-open mouths, golden suns, and silvery moons flying all around.

And the torrent of noises that whistled and crackled, squeaked, squealed, buzzed, and jingled from every nook and cranny caused the spectators to forget, almost, the colorful panorama about them. Anyone capable of handling a musical instrument was playing it wholeheartedly. Long-necked two-string guitars, small drums, and slender oboe-like reed instruments competed with the pipes and castanets as to which could make the biggest noise. The people who didn't belong among the musicians shook their growling, rasping rattles. And to make the cacophony complete, everyone was singing at the top of his lungs, each one a different favorite tune.

The crowds and the deafening noises seemed to please Mr. Grimes very much. Jan had expected him, a real, brisk American, to be impatient at having to crawl forward at such a slow pace, but for the first time since his arrival, Mr. Grimes began to display a broad smile. He stood up in the jeep, observing with great delight the masses of people making their way down to the riverbank. At times he waved his straw hat in sheer jubilation.

After Mr. Grimes had had a shower in his room and rejoined the group waiting for him on the hotel's terrace, Jan found out why the masses of people, the colors, and the babble of noise had made the master driller so happy. Mr. Grimes told them that this was the tenth anniversary of his employment with Aramco. Aramco is an abbreviation for the Arabian-American Company, the huge oil outfit that is developing the vast oil fields in Saudi Arabia. For nearly ten years, Mr. Grimes, together with several geologists, engineers, and electrical workers, had roamed the desert under the pro-

tection of a group of Arabian soldiers and had made about fifty test diggings at different locations.

"We never met other people unless we chanced to cross paths with a Bedouin caravan," the master driller said, "and those encounters weren't any pleasure. In spite of the romantic stuff you see in the movies, the Bedouins are simply primitive, nomadic shepherds and camel raisers. And to top it all, they smell rather badly, too," he concluded with a little laugh.

"Each time we finally finished a series of test diggings, we returned to Aramco's big oil refineries and spent several days there, where we had all the comforts of civilization—from showers to movies—but the only thing we missed was real liveliness. In the compounds, there were only the employees, people who had come there to work and to earn money but not to live, really. No one can stand the heat and the dry climate for more than a few years, after which they move on to an assignment elsewhere or just up and quit."

"But didn't you ever get any time off to go back to America for a visit?" Jan inquired.

"Oh yes, of course. We were allowed six weeks' vacation time per year, plus a round-trip plane ticket to the States at a reduced rate. But after those six weeks, it was even more difficult to return to the inferno of the desert—especially if you have a wife and children at home."

"I assume you have a wife and children," Hans said.

"Look here," Grimes answered, taking out a large bunch of color photographs from his wallet. "This is my wife, and these are Peter and Paul, our boys. One of them is about your age," he said, pointing at Jan. "However, he has freckles," he added, beaming with fatherly pride.

"But if you're going to stick around Thailand a while and the family is going to remain in America, you'll have to wait a long time before you see them again, won't you?" Jan said.

"Everything has been arranged," Mr. Grimes explained. "My family is arriving on the next plane from the United States, and they'll stay here until October, when the boys have to go back to school. Moreover, this job in Thailand can scarcely last more than a year—it's just a few wells. And the temperature here seems almost cool after Saudi Arabia. In addition, I've made up my mind that when I'm through here, I'm going home to the States for good. Aramco pays very well, and I've been able to save a good bit in these ten years. I've been thinking of starting a construction company or something like that back home when I've done my job on these wells."

"Would you mind if I asked you a question?" Jan said.

"Ask ahead. If it's something I don't care to answer, I'll say so."

"Well, if you're so anxious to get home to the United States and you've already saved a good bit, why did you take on this job in Thailand? The World Health Organization is not noted for its high salaries."

"Well, that's a good question," Mr. Grimes replied, but not without a slight hint of irritation. "You seem to be under the illusion that we Americans are not interested in anything that doesn't pay a lot of money. It may be hard for you to imagine, but I, too, would like to do something to help the underdeveloped countries. Actually, I can tell you that what the World Health Organization is going to pay me here will cover very little besides my hotel bill and some of my food. But I took the job because I'd like to do my part in seeing

that these small children here have a little pure drinking
water. I can't believe that Mr. Nittel has come to Bangkok
just to make money, either."

Dusk was beginning to fall, and the people of Bangkok
were homeward bound from the celebration. Small yellow
taxis honked their horns in the streets, the open-air streetcars
were ringing their bells, and the ricksha boys shouted long
and loud to clear the way. People crowded into outdoor cafés
and restaurants, and the jukebox music from the tearooms
brayed out loudly into the streets. Everything was resplend-
ent and seething with life, and the fast-approaching darkness had not yet obliterated the deep green of the bushes and
the splendor of the flowers. Mr. Grimes had truly chosen the
right city in which to find relaxation and something different
after his ten years in the sterile desert sand.

Chapter Six

❖❖❖❖

SCARFACE POPS UP AGAIN

The following day the Grimes family arrived in Bangkok via Pan American Airways, and a radiant Mr. Grimes took the next day off to celebrate the reunion with his family. But on the morning of the third day, he reported ready to work out at the construction site. By the time Jan arrived by bicycle that afternoon, he found the engineer, the master driller, and Snit hard at work. They went through the contents of the five packing cases, which Grimes sorted out with both satisfaction and knowledge. An inventory showed that the sixth case, which had been sent "by mistake" to Rangoon, contained only the platform for the drilling tower. And to the great joy of Hans and the boys, Mr. Grimes explained that they could certainly get along with a temporary bamboo platform while waiting for the other packing case to be returned from Rangoon. This temporary platform could be built sturdily enough so that they could at least get the drilling going. Before they had reached any great depth, there might be time to get the metal platform back again.

But in order to get on with the work, Mr. Grimes needed laborers, first of all to help with the platform, and then to help with the various functions of the drilling machinery. Immediately, Hans started the jeep and went into the city to talk with the Public Health Service about employing three workers from the city. Hardly an hour had passed before he was back again, reporting happily that the people at the Public Health Service office had been especially obliging and had promised to send three workers to the site the very next day.

That evening Mr. Grimes invited Hans and the Grundvahl family to dinner at his hotel. Of course, Snit was invited, too, but he begged off, explaining that he didn't dare leave all the expensive apparatus unguarded. In no time, Mrs. Grundvahl and Mrs. Grimes were good friends. Jan liked Mrs. Grimes, too, but he was a bit skeptical as far as Peter and Paul were concerned.

When Peter and Paul learned that Snit was unable to come to dinner because he had to guard the installation, they wanted to go out there immediately to meet him and Dog and to take them some ice cream. It was with great difficulty that Mr. Grimes and Hans managed to talk them into postponing this trip until the next day.

The meeting was a pretty stormy one, at least for Snit. The American boys practically knocked poor Snit down, and he was utterly speechless in the presence of the lively foreigners. Peter and Paul were not content merely with repeated handshakes—in themselves more than enough for Snit, who wasn't accustomed to this manner of greeting—but they also boxed him playfully in the stomach, as was their American habit, and tried to slap him on the shoulders and back. Finally, Snit had had enough and withdrew from the scene, his feelings clearly hurt. It was up to Jan to explain to the astonished boys how very much the Thailanders dislike being touched by others and to tell them that what was a sign of friendliness in their country was a sign of contempt and inferiority here in Thailand.

After a while, Jan managed to persuade Snit that the two boys were not trying to tease or kill him. Peter and Paul themselves pitched in and said repeatedly that they were sorry. Moreover, their facial expressions showed clearly that they were truly concerned over the misunderstanding. At last, Snit began to laugh, and peace was restored. The tacit agreement was completed when Peter and Paul let Snit examine their freckles, a phenomenon that the young Thailander had never before observed. Snit asked Jan if the freckles were some sort of sign of aristocracy in the U.S.A. Laughing uproariously, Peter and Paul explained that the freckles weren't a sign of anything whatsoever, but Snit's question was the motivation behind the nicknames that were bestowed upon the American boys that day and that they were to carry the entire time they were there. From that moment on, they were Freckles I and Freckles II, and that was that.

It didn't take long to discover that the Freckles boys were complete failures at table tennis—and they weren't in the least ashamed of this fact. On the other hand, they were, they assured Jan and Snit, the best football players in their classes at home—not the ordinary European soccer, called football, but American football, in which an oval ball is driven from goal to goal with both hands and feet, accompanied by fierce battles. Jan had seen American football in the movies and on television, and he remarked immediately that football was no sport but, rather, a mass battle and nothing else. This observation led to a long drawn-out argument between Jan and the Freckles boys, but before the discussion turned into something resembling American football, Jan maneuvered the subject of conversation to more

peaceful grounds by offering to teach the Freckles boys to play table tennis. This offer strengthened the friendship among the four boys, especially after Peter and Paul gave Snit a present—a spyglass in a leather case, which they happened to have with them.

Snit, utterly delighted with his treasure, spent a good fifteen minutes just looking at things through it. From that time forward, every now and then he would hold it to his eye.

While the boys were getting acquainted with one another, Mr. Grimes had begun working in earnest. It was soon evident that enormous energy and working power lay hidden beneath the modest, unassuming expression of the American —not to mention the specialized knowledge he was able to bring to bear. As Jan watched Mr. Grimes at work, he realized how the U.S.A. had acquired its opulence and become one of the world's great powers. The three Thai workers, naked from the waist up, were dragged along at his furious pace, and soon the perspiration began to drip from their naked backs because of the unusual working tempo. People who live in tropical climates usually move slowly by instinct. Even their dances are slow, and you seldom, if ever, see a violent gesture.

Mr. Grimes marked the bamboo poles, which were about five or six inches in diameter, at the proper length, after which the workers sawed off the ends. Each pole was over nineteen feet long. Then Mr. Grimes and Hans placed markers where each bamboo pole was to be placed around the digging site and told the workers to dig a hole about eighteen inches deep at each of these places. After Mr. Grimes had prepared a thick cement mixture, the poles were embedded in it in the holes. Finally, they pushed the poles inward at just the right angle for their upper ends to cross, as if this were the framework for a gigantic tent.

The bamboo platform, which had been designed as a temporary support for the drilling tower, was finished the first

day. The following day Mr. Grimes had the workers con-
struct a platform of smaller bamboo poles and put it right
beside the drilling tower. On top of that platform, they made
a floor of planks with a small bamboo ladder leading up to
it. Bamboo is not an easy material to work with, but each of
the three workers was a master at the art of sawing it and
nailing it together. Even greater mastery was needed when
it came to fastening the poles one to another. It was not possible to screw them together, because bamboo poles are hol-
low, and the seemingly tough outer surface is easily splin-
tered. For this reason, the workers fastened the joints where
the poles and the platform met with thin but very strong
jute ropes, doing all this with such skill that the smooth, slippery poles didn't move a fraction of an inch, even when
loaded to the hilt. This is an art which is thousands of years
old in Thailand and in all the countries of the Far East where
bamboo is abundant.

The four boys were always eager to help, but Snit had the
art of making himself especially useful. To be sure, his broad
shoulders and stocky figure hinted at enormous physical
strength, but even so, Jan and the Freckles boys were astonished time after time when they saw how effortlessly he lifted
the long bamboo poles. In addition, he had a real talent for
climbing. He would merely shake off his sandals and, like a
monkey, shinny up the slippery bamboo poles. Jan, regarded
as a good gymnast at home in Sweden, tried to repeat Snit's
performance but couldn't manage it at all. He just couldn't
get a grip on the smooth surface, and after two or three yards
he would slip down again.

Finally the powerful, tentlike drilling tower was ready,
along with the platform and its steps. Now it was just a ques-

tion of getting the apparatus on top of the platform. Just a
question? It didn't take them long to discover that this was
much easier said than done. To begin with, Mr. Grimes had
to attach a steel hook in the fork where the poles met. Then
came a pulley and a long chain. Then the boys and workers,
using all the strength they could muster, hauled load after
load up with the pulley, until all the parts of the apparatus
were on the platform. Once they were up, Hans helped Mr.
Grimes assemble the parts, but even though Mr. Grimes had
organized the whole maneuver so well and though each did
his utmost in the way of work, it took two whole afternoons
to get everything in place.

Finally, Mr. Grimes took out a handkerchief about the
size of a sheet, wiped the perspiration from his forehead and
neck, and said, "Tomorrow we'll assemble the actual bore
and get going."

The Grundvahls and Grimeses were out in full force for
the ceremonies marking the initiation, and the ladies saw
that there was no lack of refreshing soft drinks. Furthermore,
they had on hand a great many tempting sandwiches in covered baskets. Even Mr. Grimes, who had certainly initiated
many diggings in his lifetime, looked a little pompous when
he got the apparatus going and watched the drill head beginning to sink into the soft earth as he pressed on the instrument controls. Everything functioned as it should. The newly
lubricated parts whirred away without the platform's moving
an inch, and soon the first length of the bore disappeared
under the surface.

Besides the other employees and their families, the ceremonies had drawn an appreciable audience. At least a hundred people, men, women, and children, had gathered at the

barbed-wire fence, and when the whir of the machinery
became audible, there was spontaneous applause. Hans hurried over to the entrance and let them inside the area, an
action that Mr. Grimes didn't seem too pleased over. At
length, Snit confessed to Jan that it was he who had spread
the word about what was going on when he had been out the
previous afternoon shopping for food, which explained how
the audience had been able to assemble at just the right time.

After the digging, Snit mentioned casually that the river
was about to overflow its banks. It had rained much more
than usual the previous week—at times the heavy clouds
gathered not once but twice a day, accompanied each time
by torrential rains.

Under the circumstances, it was not the least unusual for
the river to begin to rise, but Jan became somewhat concerned since this meant that they might have to postpone
their swimming excursion the following Sunday. The
Freckles boys consoled him by saying that, in the event of
postponement, they could swim instead at the hotel, where
there was a blue-tile pool seventy-five feet long.

The boys had experienced a rather unpleasant episode
some days earlier at the swimming pool. One morning the
Freckles boys had invited Jan and Snit to come swimming
with them, and all four of them had dressed in the Grimeses'
suite and gone directly down to the pool. Before they had
had a chance to stick their toes in the water, one of the hotel
porters in his dark-blue uniform with gold trimmings had
suddenly appeared. Without a word he pointed first at Snit
and then at the exit. Even in Europe a well-bred person
doesn't point at another person, but in Thailand this is regarded as a deep insult. Snit's face grew pale.

Peter and Paul, however, were not the sort of boys who kept their peace at a suggestion of this sort.

"What's the problem?" they said almost simultaneously in less than friendly voices.

"The use of the swimming pool is restricted to the guests of the hotel, and that youngster isn't one of them!"

"If no one but the guests of the hotel can use the swimming pool, why didn't you object to our other friend here?" Peter broke in. He didn't like having the porter refer to Snit as a "youngster."

The angry Freckles boys didn't bother to wait for an answer but headed straight for a door in the corridor marked "The Manager." You could almost guess what happened in there, because a short time later the door opened again, the hotel manager himself came over to Snit, and, with much bowing, begged his pardon and assured Mr. Labanukors that he was welcome at any and all times to use the hotel's swimming pool whenever he pleased. A short time after the manager had disappeared, the uniformed porter reappeared and apologized, with concealed anger, to both Snit and the Freckles boys. With that, the episode was over, and the boys splashed around happily in the pool for the remainder of the morning.

That evening as they were eating, Jan told the story to his father.

"Well, that's the way things are in most of the African and Asian countries. The ones who have climbed up a few steps on the so-called social ladder act very condescendingly and ill-manneredly toward their own countrymen. You see this so often with subordinate public and private servants. The porter, of course, realized that Snit didn't belong to the 'upper class' and wanted, therefore, to put him in his place."

As a result of this, Jan and Snit didn't have much desire to use the swimming pool from then on. They were a little downhearted, therefore, at the thought of the waters rising enough so that their Sunday swimming excursion would go up in smoke. The construction site lay at the foot of a hill a good distance from the river, which meant that it was in no immediate danger. Just to be on the safe side, however, the boys walked down to the banks to check on the motorboat and to take a look at the high waters.

The huge river, which usually flowed along rather sluggishly, was now moving much more rapidly, and the color of the water had changed from yellow to almost brown. Large whirlpools could be seen here and there on the surface, and the current carried along with it both branches and huge tree stumps. The water had already begun to overflow into the floors of the houses on poles, and the small canals leading to the nearby rice fields had been obliterated, so that the whole surface now resembled a level mirror of water. Snit informed them that if the rice plants got too much water, they would drown and, of course, stop growing. Because of this, the farmers were always very careful to see that the tops of the tender plants were above the water. Flooding would surely ruin the rice harvest, Snit explained.

For safety's sake, the motor for the boat was kept up at the construction site. Therefore, it wasn't very difficult for the four boys to drag the boat out of the water and, as insurance against the unexpected, tie it to a large tree a little higher up.

At the construction site, Mr. Grimes carried on his tireless work. On the fourth day, water suddenly began to spring up through the hole, causing Snit, who happened to be helping at the machinery, to give a spontaneous shout of joy. He soon quieted down, however, when he realized that Mr. Grimes was more gloomy than glad. Hans explained to him that the digging had now reached the subsoil water, which was springing up so suddenly. But this water was just as polluted as that in the older wells already in existence. The fact that you had found water a few yards below the surface didn't mean that you had neared your goal, because there was much work to be done before reaching the clean, clear water they were after.

During the next few days, the river waters rose even higher, and often you could see parts of houses and animal bodies floating on the crests of the waves. The boys had to go down and bring the boat to even higher ground, and when they got there, they found to their amazement that the fields near the banks were inundated and that the slimy waves had pushed much higher than before.

Snit told them that the floods had caused a good deal of tension and unhappiness in the residential section where he usually bought his food. The old ladies cried and complained; the men spoke bitterly of the number of people who had starved to death when previous floods had ruined the rice harvest. With folded hands, the men sat on their balconies looking gloomily at the rising waters. Of course, there wasn't a thing they could do about the flooding. In the nearby temples, women gathered twenty-four hours a day, kneeling before the statues of Buddha, offering gifts of flowers and pleading for delivery from the danger that was threatening them.

Hans took a more practical view of the matter.

"In the future, they will have to control the river by building up the banks high enough to take care of this," he said to the boys. "If they don't do this, they'll be in for floods again as soon as heavier than ordinary rains come. There are so many things to be done, both here in Thailand and in the other underdeveloped countries. Generations of neglect can't be repaired in one day," he said.

One afternoon while Snit was working on the platform of the drilling tower in company with Mr. Grimes and one of the workers, he suddenly picked up his telescope, which he always carried around his neck, and put it to his eye. He stood for a while staring unremittingly down at the road.

"Mr. Grimes, a big crowd of people from the residential quarters is coming this way," he reported.

"Let them come and get yourself busy with something useful," Mr. Grimes grumbled. "What do we care what they do?"

It was soon evident, however, that Mr. Grimes was going to have to care very much what they were doing. Several hundred people were heading straight for the construction site, and even from a good distance, you could see that many of them were shouting and waving their fists menacingly. Their facial expressions revealed hate, bitterness, and hostility.

Mr. Grimes and the worker climbed down from the platform, leaving Snit alone there, still with the telescope to his eye.

"Hans," Snit suddenly cried. "The one who is carrying on the most violently is a monk right in the middle of the crowd with a scar on the left side of his face."

"Scarface!" the boys shouted almost simultaneously. "The

mysterious Scarface who got hold of our sixth case and had it shipped out!"

Soon the crowd had reached the enclosure. The people farther back pushed against the ones up near the fence, which had not been designed to withstand pressure of this sort. One of the poles broke in two with a loud crack, and the crowd swarmed onto the site. Hans, the three workers, Mr. Grimes, and the boys instinctively backed up toward the barrack entrance.

Mr. Grimes, speaking very softly, said to Hans, who was right beside him, "Go after some weapons, Hans, and I'll try to stave off the crowd with the revolver, at least for a while."

"For heaven's sake," Hans said, "don't get out a revolver. If they catch sight of it, they'll just get more uncontrollable. Let me try to calm them down instead."

Several of the crowd, instead of approaching the retreating employees, went over to the drilling tower and tried to break down the solid bamboo poles. Among them was a monk in a saffron-yellow robe, with a scar on his left cheek.

Hans positioned himself at the entrance steps, lifted his arms in order to quiet them down, and then said in a powerful voice, "Why do you come here this way and try to damage the installation? A few of you will have to step up and tell me what you have in mind."

Their answer came in the form of angry oaths and hostile words, but Hans didn't allow himself to be intimidated. Instead, he raised his arms once more.

"That doesn't explain a thing." Then, pointing at a man in the first row, he turned directly to him. "We know each other, you and I. You were the one who got an empty gasoline can from me just a few days ago. Step forward and speak up. What is it you want?"

The man stepped forward and began speaking in a voice that almost shook with emotion.

"We want you to stop this evil work immediately and get your machinery out of here!"

"That's right. What he said is right. Get this hellish machinery out of here!" hundreds of voices said in chorus.

"But why do you want us to move our machinery out of here?" Hans asked in amazement.

"You are in league with the spirits of the devil," a thin female voice shouted.

"Just a minute," Hans said. "Do you think our drilling machinery has caused the floods? Whoever put an idea like that into your heads?"

"They've lost their senses entirely!" Mr. Grimes said. "Never in my twenty years as master driller have I seen the like of this."

"A monk has told us. One of our holy men told us that Buddha doesn't want people drilling holes in the earth. The monk gave us a message from the abbot and told us that we should destroy the machinery," shouted the excited voices of the crowd.

"I see. A monk told you," Hans repeated. "Well, then, let him come up to me himself and say it right to my face— that is, if he dares to."

The crowd seemed to approve of his suggestion.

"Come forth, honorable monk, and tell the words of truth to the *farang*," people cried out from all directions.

But the cries and admonishments were in vain. The monk had suddenly disappeared. The crowd searched for him, looking all around the area, but the monk in the yellow robe was not there. Even Snit, who had tried to keep an eye on him every second, had not seen him leave the construction site.

"Naturally, I could have been mistaken," he said softly to Jan.

"Here's his robe," a man cried out suddenly, picking up a long saffron-yellow garment, which he found behind a pile of pipes. The crowd, so recently excited, seemed to have calmed down a bit. A few hurried over to get a closer look at the yellow robe, others argued back and forth as to what it all meant, and still others began to take leave of the site.

Hans noticed the changed atmosphere.

"Don't leave yet," he cried. "Listen first to what I have to say. I must talk with you."

At that point he descended the steps and got right into the midst of the crowd. Turning to an elderly man, he directed a question to him.

"Now, you're an old man who has seen and experienced a good deal in life, I imagine. Do you remember floods in the past?"

"Of course I do. When I was no older than the boy there" —he pointed at Snit—"the water was so high that time that it reached all the way to the royal palace. And six years ago we had such a bad flood that two of my best buffaloes drowned. That year there wasn't a grain of rice in the whole district."

"Now, you see. The river has overflowed many times before," Hans said, "long before we came here to dig wells for you. Isn't that true? Isn't it true that the river always over-flows its banks when the rains have been too heavy?"

"Naturally, it happens that way," the old man replied. "It

always overflows when the rains have been heavier than usual."

"That may be, but the monk said to us that Buddha doesn't want people digging holes in the earth in any case," a stubborn woman remarked. "And it was the abbot himself who decreed that we should destroy your hellish machinery."

"Let me make a suggestion," Hans said. "Choose three persons whom everyone respects—men or women—and I'll take them with me to the abbot and hear what he has to say about the matter."

After brief deliberations, the crowd, now appreciably smaller and quite calm, picked two men and a woman as their representatives. Hans got into the jeep with them and drove straight to the cloister. Within half an hour, they had returned to the construction site, during which time the rebellious masses had turned into peaceful neighbors who had quietly begun to return to their homes. A number of them asked Snit to tell Mr. Grimes that they would gladly repair the fence. Others merely bowed deeply and went their way. The remainder of them sneaked off shamefacedly.

While Hans was at the cloister, Mr. Grimes and the boys tried to determine whether or not the mob had managed to damage the machinery. Apart from several knife marks, the bamboo poles seemed solid enough, and the machinery appeared to be all right. But Jan intuitively felt that there was more to the story than met the eye. After the others had finished their examination, he stayed by the machines and inspected them inch by inch. At the precise point where the double screw of the machine fastened the pipes together, he discovered a small packet not much larger than the palm of his hand, which someone had attached to an almost inaccessible place on the inner surface. Mr. Grimes noticed that Jan had come upon something and took the small packet out of his hand.

"Why, the dirty rats!" he stormed. "These are dynamite cartridges. If we had started up the machinery, the whole thing would have exploded in seconds, blowing us and the drilling machinery into thin air. We've got to tell the police about this! Those dirty saboteurs!"

"I'm sure it was Scarface," Snit declared. "I saw him sneaking around the machine, but I didn't know what he was up to!"

"Well, a very nice monk he was!" Mr. Grimes sneered angrily. "A monk trying to blow people up! You'll have to be a witness for the police, Snit. Blackguards dressed in gold. Instead of giving us their help and being grateful to us for our efforts, they're trying to blow us and the machinery up!"

Once Hans had returned, however, it was clear that Mr. Grimes's suspicions about the monks were quite groundless. The abbot had solemnly assured them that he had not sent a message to any of the people in the suburb telling them to destroy the digging installation and to blow up the machines. On the contrary, he gave his blessing to the great work the *farangs* were doing and to their unselfish efforts.

And no one in the entire cloister had a scar on his cheek. No one had ever heard tell of a monk with such a scar.

Chapter Seven

❖❖❖

DOG GOES INTO ACTION

That same evening Hans, Mr. Grimes, and the boys held a large planning session out at the site. Mr. Grundvahl had been invited. The question before the assembly was whether or not they should inform the police what had happened. Hans, on the one side, was a little dubious, since he was anxious to avoid all distractions such as questioning and protocol —anything that would cause them to lose a lot of working time. Mr. Grimes, on the other hand, had had rather unpleasant contacts with the Saudi Arabian authorities and police, but feeling quite sure in his own mind that the Thai police just *had* to be somewhat better than their Saudi Arabian counterparts, he suggested that they turn to the police despite everything and ask them to track down and arrest the fake monk.

It was Mr. Grundvahl who ended the debate by voting in favor of informing the police. He pointed out that Scarface had clearly demonstrated that he was out to stop them at any cost and that, for this reason, he himself would have to be stopped in time. And since they themselves were unable to do anything about him, they had to turn to the police for help.

Time and time again, the conversation turned to the puzzling question of what lay behind all these events. For his part, Jan agreed with his father, saying that there couldn't be any doubt that the same person, Scarface, was back of the robbery as well as the misdirection of the sixth packing case, the inciting of the mob, and the dynamite attempt.

"But who is this mysterious Scarface?" Mr. Grimes said. "And why does he want to keep us from digging wells?"

"Well, that's the sixty-four-dollar question, which we've got to puzzle out," Jan insisted, with the Freckles boys in staunch agreement.

"All well and good, but it's up to the police to figure that one out. Only in children's books do young boys perform brave deeds and heroically catch the thief while the police run all around on the wrong track," Mr. Grundvahl said.

Finally, Mr. Grimes, Hans, and Mr. Grundvahl got into the jeep and drove to the police station. Scarcely had they left the gate when Snit turned to the other boys.

"I've got something to show you!" he said eagerly. Without waiting for a reply, he shoved the other boys into his room, where he took out a long piece of saffron-yellow fabric that he had hidden under his mattress.

"Scarface's robe!" Jan cried. "Where did you get hold of it?"

"I took it out of the hands of the man who found it behind the pile of pipes. No one paid any attention to me at the time because everyone was just standing around listening to Hans, oblivious of anything else. Then I sneaked into my room and hid the robe under the mattress," Snit explained, obviously pleased with himself.

"But what good is this going to do? So we've laid hands

on the robe that the fake monk had on!" said one of the Freckles boys. "Did you think we might be able to use it for a masquerade costume or something of the sort?"

"In that case, you'd have to shave those carrot-colored curls off your heads first," Jan interrupted.

Snit merely remained silent. He sat there with his eyes half closed, thinking so hard that you could almost see and hear the wheels going around.

Finally, Jan said to him, "It seems to me that you have some special plan for this gold robe. Do you want to tell us what you have in mind?"

"Gladly," Snit replied happily. "I have a plan whereby we can use the dog to get Scarface."

Snit's statement was followed by a moment of astonished silence, after which Freckles I said with great delight, "I get it! Congratulations, Snit. That's a marvelous idea!"

Freckles II and Jan resembled human question marks, failing to see anything brilliant at all in the idea of using Dog in the fight against Scarface.

"Well, nobody could ever accuse you of being quick-witted," Freckles I said in a superior tone of voice. "Don't you catch on? Snit means that we'll let the dog smell the clothing and then turn him loose so that he can follow Scarface's trail. I'm positive that he can track down the skunk wherever he's hiding. The idea is great!"

At length Jan and Freckles II fathomed what Snit was up to. Jan also felt that the idea was brilliant and gave his enthusiastic approval, but Freckles II, who was a little jealous because his brother's mind functioned more quickly than his own, raised a few objections.

"But what if the hound refuses to follow the trail? You've

got to keep in mind that he's a pretty ordinary mutt, not a trained police dog. And even if he were a police dog, he would have to confine himself to working with the secret police, because the regular police would never have anything to do with a hound as forbidding as Dog is."

It was Snit's turn to be offended. Without wasting words on the outrageous allegations of Freckles II, he let out a shrill whistle, which resulted in Dog's rushing to his master, wagging his tail violently, from the corner of the site where he had been kept for the good of everyone concerned. Snit held the bundle of material and let Dog smell it inside and out. The boy waited patiently until the dog seemed at home with the smell, at which point, holding the bundle above his head, he walked over to the place where one of the demonstrators had found the garment. When they came to the pile of iron pipes, Dog scurried over to a particular spot, where he stood sniffing the ground. Once again Snit held the garment up to his nose and whispered something in his long, shaggy ear. Sniffing all the while, Dog began to head directly toward the place where the demonstrators had broken the fence pole and thronged into the enclosure. Then he headed right across the meadow toward the country road. The boys had a hard time keeping up with him.

Alongside the road, Dog halted and began to circle around in an area of about a square yard, but finally he caught the scent again. It seemed to lead directly into the center of the city along the sandy edge of the road. Dusk was falling when Dog, still sniffing and accompanied by the four boys, reached the business district.

Here the traffic seemed to make the dog hesitate again. Stopping time after time, he pressed his nose closer, if pos-

sible, to the ground and sniffed wildly. In some manner, he
managed every single time to find the trail again, showing
his delight with faint little barks. He dragged the boys with
him around several corners, and the people stared wide-eyed
at the three white boys and one Thai lad so eagerly following
the ugly dog trailing the scent.

All of a sudden the dog stopped outside the entrance to a
two-story building. No matter how hard Snit tried to get
the dog to move on, Dog replied with impatient barking, irritated over his master's retarded powers of comprehension.
Snit, not retarded at all of course, soon realized that the dog
wanted someone to open the gate for him, which was when
the boys, taking a good look at the building, discovered that
they were standing outside a police precinct office.

It was a moment of triumph for Paul who, even out at the
construction site, had expressed grave doubts over the dog's
ability as a tracker.

"There! You can see for yourselves, you guys. The dumb
dog has been following Hans's and Mr. Grundvahl's tracks
and has led us right to the police. This is really some dis-
covery!"

Snit wouldn't even condescend to exchange words with
Freckles II, but he had to admit that he was rather surprised
that the trail had led to the police. In any event, he opened
the gate, and the dog shot through like an arrow. With his
head down to the pavement, he ran through a long corridor
leading to a courtyard, on either side of which were low bar-
racks-like wings with doors and windows facing the court.
The dog smelled his way diagonally across the gravel-cov-
ered yard and, without the least hesitation, went straight up
to one of the doors, all the while with the boys at his heels.

Seemingly, the police had stopped work for the day, because no one even tried to stop them.

Finally, Dog stopped outside a door, whining and looking at Snit as if he wanted the door opened for him. Instead, however, Snit merely read the small sign on the door—*Adul Suthichoti, Police Lieutenant*—and told the other boys what he had found. A couple of yards from the door was a window with a small beam of light emanating from it out onto the courtyard. The boys went over to the window, cautiously peering into the office. Behind a simple desk sat a uniformed middle-aged man whose bald head shone in the light from a desk lamp. Absorbed in his reading, he was puffing absentmindedly on a cigarette. He sat with his head bent so far forward that no light from the lamp fell on his face. But suddenly he raised his head and reached for something on the shelf alongside the desk, at which point his round brown face came into full view.

The boys almost gasped in astonishment, because on the policeman's left cheek was a large, straight scar.

Jan pulled himself together first. Hastily, he whispered to Snit, "Hey, call the dog again. We all know that it wouldn't be very pleasant if Scarface discovered us here."

He led the way back across the courtyard, through the corridor, and off toward the gate. But it was all Snit could do to get Dog to move. From his point of view, it must have seemed strange that they had goaded him into tracking something down for so long and then, when he had finally found what he was looking for, not even praised his skill by letting him take a nip at the culprit—just a small bite on the leg.

Trembling, they found their way to the street once more

and were soon on the way to the main path. After they had gotten around the corner, Snit said, "Well, I guess that proves it. Dog is not so dumb!"

Freckles II blushed so hard that the redness even showed through his freckles, but his American sense of fair play won, and he bent down to Dog, saying, "I'm sorry, doggie." He even wanted to shake hands with Dog, who stood there staring at him with his head cocked to one side.

At this point, Snit said good-by to the others, since he had to return and begin his guard duty at the construction site. Arriving there, he was greeted with a new surprise. A policeman, armed with a machine gun, was posted at the entrance and refused to let him in. After interminable explanations, he finally cleared the way. The boy was not spiteful by nature, and when he had prepared his simple evening meal, he went out to the policeman and asked if he were hungry.

They shared a bowl of rice and vegetables, and while they were eating, the policeman admitted to Snit that he hadn't the slightest idea why he had been assigned to duty at the entrance of the construction site. All he knew was that the captain on duty had summoned him and given him his orders. He went on to say that three *farangs* had been in with the captain then and that they must have been there for quite some time because the ashtrays were almost spilling over.

Once Snit had left for the construction site, Jan and the Freckles boys held a council of war. They were in complete agreement that they shouldn't delay telling Hans, Mr. Grimes, and Mr. Grundvahl what they had discovered, so they took off for the tennis club in the hope of finding them.

As luck would have it, the men were there, and Jan told them what they had found out.

When Jan had finished his account, Mr. Grimes suddenly expressed his feelings in a very practical way. Hailing a waiter in a white jacket, he said, "Would you please go and get me a couple of good large bones, preferably some on which there is a good bit of meat left."

Turning to the others, he continued, "Those bones are my reward for the dog, and now I'm going to find something appropriate for Snit, too. That lad is a fine, conscientious fellow, and he'll go far. And now, gentlemen, I think we'd better get in touch with the police captain again. It's of utmost importance that we get the man with the scar on his face behind bars as quickly as possible. All I hope is that the good captain is not in cahoots with the criminal."

Mr. Grimes rose from the table, clearly ready to head for the police station, but Mr. Grundvahl stopped him.

"Wait a minute, George," he said calmly. "I believe we'd better think things through a little first. We have enough time, because I'm sure the captain has left his office by this time. The first question that concerns me is whether the boys might have been mistaken."

"Positively not," all three boys protested in chorus. "We are sure that the police lieutenant is the fake monk. We saw the scar he has on his left cheek very plainly. And Dog led us straight to him . . ."

They were so eager and excited that they all were speaking at once.

"Yes, I believe you," Mr. Grundvahl said, raising his hand. "But it seems peculiar to me that the police would allow one of their own men to incite people to riot against those who merely want to do some good for their country. What do you say, Hans?"

"To tell the truth, I don't understand any of it," Hans replied. "Ever since I got here, all the officials I've had anything to do with have been very polite and helpful. And I can't believe for a moment that the police captain is involved," he continued, turning to Mr. Grimes. "His annoyance this afternoon at being told what had happened out at the site couldn't have been put on. And he immediately arranged for a police guard to go on duty out there."

"How can you be so sure that he wasn't just being a good actor?" Mr. Grimes said suspiciously. "How do we know that the guard they sent out isn't in the same league?"

The discussion went on for a while, but finally they all agreed that the following day Hans should call on the police captain in his office, taking the three Caucasian boys with him. They did not include Snit because they knew he wanted no contact with the police after his previous experiences. Were the police captain to order an investigation, Snit could be called on later as a witness.

The next morning Hans, Jan, and the Freckles boys gathered outside police headquarters. This building was in a different part of the city from the station where the boys had discovered Scarface the day before and, in addition, was much larger. The police captain seemed a bit surprised, but he received them pleasantly. His countenance, however, darkened noticeably when Hans told him what the boys had discovered.

"Well, that sounds very interesting, indeed," he said coldly, "but you'll have to admit that it all seems very peculiar. Here you are, accusing a police officer, first, of disguising himself as a harbor official and ordering one of your cases back on the ship; secondly, you say he disguised himself as a monk and incited the crowd against you, trying, at the same time, to blow up the construction site. Can you come forth with a sensible explanation as to why he should have done all these things?"

That question had been discussed endlessly the night before, and Hans was unable to suggest a logical reason.

"Furthermore," the police captain continued, "you're accusing a public servant of several serious crimes. And the only grounds for these accusations are that these young boys think they recognized the police lieutenant as the fake monk."

"Our age has nothing to do with the matter!" one of the Freckles boys complained.

"Perhaps not," the police captain replied, turning to Hans, "but the fact is that I know Lieutenant Suthichoti very well. He has been on the force for ten years, and heretofore there has never been one complaint against him. He is a proper, capable member of the forces of law and order. And now you come down here with three children who think they have enough grounds to cause me to arrest him!"

"We didn't ask any such thing!" Hans answered. "But I did think it was my civic duty to inform you of the new development in the case. And I do have the right to demand that you investigate the matter, and I *am* demanding that much!"

"You have no right to demand anything whatsoever, Engineer Nittel," replied the police captain caustically. "It is my business exclusively to evaluate your information and, in line with my own opinion of its worth, to take the steps I feel necessary. Is that clear?"

In anger, Hans got up and prepared to leave. But Jan stood in his way and, in a soft voice, pleaded with him to stay for a minute or two. Then he himself talked to the police captain.

"Captain, I realize that you don't want to believe our story," he said. "And I must admit that the whole thing sounds pretty hard to believe. But I assure you we are telling the truth. Therefore, I ask only that you summon the lieutenant here and ask him where he was between two and three o'clock yesterday afternoon."

The police captain was clearly impressed by Jan's calm, polite way of speaking. Dropping at once his gruff, unfriendly manner, he replied, "I'd be glad to, young man. Just to calm your fears and to keep our relationship a good one, I'll be glad to grant your wish and ask Lieutenant Suthichoti where he was yesterday afternoon. But I will do it by telephone."

Then he took up the phone, asked to be connected to the police precinct in question, and requested to speak with Lieutenant Suthichoti. Hans and the three boys waited expectantly. Two minutes passed, then three, but the lieutenant didn't answer. Finally someone else answered. Listening attentively, the captain finally gave some instructions in a guttural tone of voice.

"Well, you tell the lieutenant to come here and see me as soon as possible today. It has to do with an official matter. Yes, that is an order. Thanks."

Turning to the four, he continued, "Lieutenant Suthichoti

didn't report for work today. Perhaps he is sick. But, as you heard, I left orders for him to come here the minute he reports in. If he reports in sick, I'll go out to his house. And I hope, gentlemen, that this will satisfy you for the moment.

Forgive me if I was a little rough, Engineer Nittel. If you want to look in this afternoon, I'll report on my conversation with the lieutenant. Now good-by, gentlemen."

His voice was very different from what it had been a little while ago when he shook hands with Hans and the boys and accompanied them to the door.

Out at the construction site, Mr. Grimes and Snit eagerly awaited their return. When Hans had finished his account of the conversation with the police captain, Mr. Grimes, infuriated, kept muttering, time after time, that procedures should have been put in motion the night before, not today.

After lunch Hans took the jeep in to police headquarters again. In no more than half an hour, he returned with the news that the lieutenant had not reported for duty and that he wasn't to be found at his residence. The captain had immediately ordered "wanted" posters put up for Scarface.

Mr. Grimes threw his hat on the ground and growled, "Wanted! Wanted! That skunk of a monk isn't so dumb as to let himself be captured like a docile child. The stupid jerks!"

In the days that followed, it seemed that Mr. Grimes was right. The inquiries yielded absolutely no result, and it seemed that Scarface had been swallowed up by the earth.

Chapter Eight

❖❖❖❖

THE DAILY ROUTINE
AND A NEW MYSTERY

There is an old Thai proverb which states that miracles never last longer than three days. This was confirmed in the matter of the fake monk with the scar. For three days, every conversation at the construction site showed a marked tendency to drift to the subject of the riot, the fake monk, and the cleverness Snit and Dog had shown. No matter how they tried to think of other things, these matters were uppermost in everyone's minds. The story might have dragged on endlessly—certainly longer than the three days called for in the proverb—if it hadn't been for an occurrence, this time a happy one.

A notice came saying that the sixth packing case had reached the Rangoon harbor in good condition and that it had been put aboard a freighter headed for Bangkok. The boat, which was called *The South Star,* was to land the next day. The news was the more welcome because Mr. Grimes had by that time begun to be a little nervous about the bamboo platform. The deeper they drilled, the more power was needed in the machine and the heavier the strain on the platform became. The solid poles were still holding, but the eagle eye of the master driller had noticed that they had begun to buckle ever so slightly under the load.

"We have only a few days to go," he had recently remarked. "Then we'll have to postpone the drilling if we don't want to run the risk of having the bamboo poles give way altogether."

Hans and the boys had received this news with great dismay. Everyone was impatiently waiting for the moment when they would reach the water strata, and Hans had already analyzed several samples of the dirt and gravel that had come up during the drilling. According to Hans's figures, they had gotten only about halfway down to the calculated depth, but there was still a possibility that the layer of stone that surrounded the water was nearer to the surface of the earth than originally estimated. They had reached the stage in drilling where tension rose day by day, as well as impatience. If they had had to call it off, even for several days, it would have been regarded as a catastrophe, except by Mr. Grimes. He had done this work for so many years that he was immune to both exaggerated expectations and deep disappointments.

"Take it easy, boys, just take it easy," he said. "All over Saudi Arabia I was known as a lucky guy. And no matter how much technique and knowledge you have, you've got to be blessed with a little luck, too."

On the arrival date of *The South Star*, the whole group waited down at the pier—except for Mr. Grimes, who explained that he couldn't interrupt his work and that he wouldn't dare leave the workers without some supervision. This was merely an excuse, the real reason being that he realized how desperately Snit wanted to go with the rest to the harbor. Had Mr. Grimes accompanied them, Snit would have been forced to stay behind at the construction site. Everyone agreed that, after what had happened, the site couldn't be left unguarded for a single moment.

With slow dignity the huge boat was maneuvered into the pier, and the unloading began immediately. The big wooden case that had given them so much trouble soon appeared among the other freight and was lowered to the ground. On this occasion they were free of difficulties, and the customs man, who knew the whole story, gave the case preference over anything else arriving.

It took two days of hard labor before they could dismantle the bamboo platform and assemble the contents of the sixth case in its place.

Rumor spread through the residential quarter nearby, and that evening a ten-man delegation arrived at the site. All were dressed in their best, and the leader of the delegation —one of those who had been most vocal during the demonstration—brought with him something wrapped in a Paisley silk cloth. Hans received the visitors with great friendliness, but Mr. Grimes mumbled something and disappeared into the barrack.

The delegation leader made a little speech in which he expressed their hopes for the steel tower, which Hans then showed to the entire company. After a great deal of ceremonious bowing, the man revealed what was hidden in the silken folds—a beautifully made silver dish that contained the greatest delicacy a Thai can conceive of—lotus seed. The lotus, which grows in warm water and has huge red and white blossoms, is Buddha's favorite flower, which is why people often decorate the statues of Buddha with lotus

blossoms and leaves. And since the lotus seed is the origin
of Buddha's favorite flower, the Thailanders endow it with
the magic powers of bestowing good fortune and peace upon
all who eat it.

Fully aware of the honor they were granting him, Hans put
several peeled lotus seeds in his mouth and, as is the custom
of the country, asked the leader of the delegation to taste the
contents of the little silver dish. The bowl was then passed
all around, and even the boys received a small share of the
seeds. It was the first time Jan had tasted the famous delicacy
responsible for the poetic name of the Thailanders—the
"lotus-eaters." The small seeds had a pleasant, somewhat
acrid flavor, which left one's mouth with a nice cool taste.
Jan was unable to see that his soul had become filled with any
special, wondrous Buddhistic peace, but still it was fun to
have tried this Thailand specialty.

Despite his great interest in the progress of the digging,
Hans had less and less time to devote to the construction site
itself. Eight additional wells were called for in the plans, and
there were many preliminaries to be accomplished so that
drilling could begin directly at the next site once it was finished at the first. The location of the second well was on the
other side of the river on a largish island separated from the
bank by a wide canal. The only way to get there was by motorboat, which meant that the craft Snit had managed to
recover was now being put to good use. Jan and the Freckles
boys often accompanied Hans on his trips to the projected
second well; by this time Jan was spending almost the whole
day at either the current or the future site. Mrs. Grundvahl
complained that she never saw her son any more except in

the morning and evening, but Mr. Grundvahl immediately came to Jan's defense.

"Don't forget that Jan has his job to look after," he said. "What's more, you can't really hope to have a man at home all the time, sitting and keeping his mother company."

The Grundvahls and Grimeses had made plans for a joint Sunday excursion. Hans and Snit had been invited, of course, but Hans explained he had already promised that Snit could have Sunday off and that he must himself stay and guard the construction site. Snit had made plans to visit his former employer, whom he hadn't seen for several weeks. They were still on good terms, and the employer's family were looking forward to seeing him.

Sunday turned out to be sunny and cloudless, and the families got into their cars and took off. On this occasion they didn't head north along the river because the waters were still high, and the yellowish brown color was not too inviting for bathing. Leaving the city, they went instead to Thonburi, a small sea resort. Here on the outskirts of the city, the cove water was blue and crystal-clear, just made for swimming. The only problem was that the warm sea water was a breeding ground for sharks, which once in a while attacked humans. To be sure, the sharks were seldom fearless enough to wander in to the beach, but it seemed safest to swim within the marked-off area, where permanently employed guards in small boats roamed the area constantly in search of the treacherous marauders of the sea.

The family excursion was a pleasant one, with no sharks to interrupt the swimming. Both families had planned to end the day by having supper together at the Grimeses' hotel and by going to a theater where a famous dance company was performing. But before they even reached the dining room, the hotel porter told them that a Mr. Snit had called and left a message that Mr. Grimes should go out to the construction site the minute he returned to the hotel. Filled with misgivings, the boys immediately begged off attending the performance, saying that they preferred to go out to the installation instead. The women had to make do with Mr. Grundvahl as their escort at supper and the theater.

Mr. Grimes made good time because the streets at that time of day were relatively empty. The boys were extremely curious as to what had happened and why Snit had called, but when they arrived, everything seemed to be in order. The lantern at the entrance to the barrack was burning as usual, and the drilling tower seemed undisturbed.

Snit met them at the entrance. He was terribly upset, and his voice seemed deeper than usual. He told them that when he had returned at six in the evening, he had not been able to find Hans anywhere. By now it was past eight, and Hans still hadn't put in an appearance. Snit was painfully conscious of their agreement never to leave the site unwatched, and for this reason he found it difficult to understand why Hans had not lived up to his part of the bargain.

Mr. Grimes did his best to maintain a calm appearance, but his steps were more rapid than usual as he walked inside the barrack and headed for Hans's room. In the study, everything seemed to be in order. On the big drawing board were the maps of well number three and some sectional enlargements that Jan had prepared in the last few days. Near the maps was a paper pad filled with numbers and marks—evidence that Hans had been on the job even on Sunday. After inspecting the barrack, Mr. Grimes went out and turned the

car toward the drilling tower. In the area illuminated by
the headlights, he inspected the entire steel structure up and
down. The machinery was subjected to the same careful inspection, but everything seemed to be as it should. Its appearance was no different from that of the previous evening.

There was nothing at all to suggest that anything extraordinary had taken place. The only thing Snit could add
was that when he came home, he had noticed that Dog
hadn't come to meet him as he generally did, eagerly wagging his tail and barking.

"Dog was actually asleep when I got here," Snit remarked.
"And he's still acting a little strangely."

Mr. Grimes hurried to the telephone and called all the
places where Hans generally ate. But the *farang* engineer
had not been seen at any of them all day. Of course, it was
possible that he had been detained on the other side of the
river.

It was a gloomy group that reassembled outside the barrack, and after a while Snit said sorrowfully, "I was positive
from the beginning that the riot and the dynamite attempt
on the tower weren't the last we were going to hear
from Scarface. I've been expecting something else, and now
poor Engineer Hans is the victim . . ."

At hearing Snit's lamentations, Mr. Grimes flew into a
rage—or at least pretended to do so. "Don't talk nonsense,"
he snorted. "Why should Hans necessarily have gotten into
trouble? He's young, boy, and maybe he's just out with some
girl. I can't understand why you're standing around moping
this way. I'm sure he'll be here ready to work in the
morning."

"I don't believe it for a minute," Snit objected in a tone of discouragement. "Engineer Hans is not the kind to leave the site unguarded just for the sake of a girl. I'm sure Scarface has been at it again."

Mr. Grimes was aware that it was pointless to continue the discussion. Finally, they decided that he would drive the Freckles boys and Jan to the hotel and come back out to spend the night at the site. Snit bravely declared that he wasn't at all afraid to stay alone there overnight, but deep down inside he was happy that the master driller had promised to come out and keep him company.

Jan didn't sleep much that night. When he met his parents at the hotel after the performance and told them that Hans had disappeared, Mr. Grundvahl's face wore a grave expression. Unlike Mr. Grimes, he didn't try to laugh it all off just to console the boys.

"All we can do for the time being is wait," he declared after a while. "But if he isn't back in the morning, I see nothing else to do but turn to the police."

The Grimes boys pointed out that the police hadn't come up with a thing on the Scarface case and that nobody yet knew where the false monk had gone. They accused the police chief outright of not *wanting* to do anything about the matter, but Mr. Grundvahl was energetic in his opposition to the statement.

"I've been asking around among my friends and acquaintances," he said, "and everyone confirms my feeling that the chief of police is an upstanding, honorable man who takes his job very seriously. It's ridiculous to imagine that the Thai officials would do anything themselves to upset the well-digging project. After all, the Thai government itself applied to the World Health Organization for hydraulic experts, and they've assisted Hans in every way with his preparations and his work so that the outcome of the project would be good."

"But why in the world would the police lieutenant with the scar try to smuggle away that sixth case, then? And why did he incite the people to demonstrate against us? Why did he try to blow up the machinery? And why has Hans disappeared all of a sudden?" The Freckles boys bombarded Mr. Grundvahl with a million questions, and he finally had to admit that he couldn't answer a single one. By that time it was very late, and the Grundvahls had to go home.

The next morning Mr. Grundvahl awakened Jan unusually early and told him to come along out to the construction site. On the way out, Jan could tell by the expression on his father's face that he took the matter seriously and was deeply upset by what had happened. No good news awaited them at the site. They didn't even need to ask if Hans had reappeared; they could tell by Mr. Grimes's expression and Snit's downcast countenance. A few moments later the Grimes boys arrived, plainly more subdued than usual. Mr. Grimes and Mr. Grundvahl, after a short conference, made up their minds that if Hans had not come back by noon, Mr. Grundvahl was going to tell the police. Then Mr. Grundvahl had to go to work.

In the shade of the barrack, the boys sat quiet and crestfallen; Mr. Grimes didn't have his heart in it when he gave the workers the sign to start the machine. At length, Jan came up with a new suggestion.

"Hey, you guys, why don't we inventory Hans's stuff and find out if anything is missing. That might lead us to something."

The room where Hans slept was easily inventoried because, apart from his books, Hans had not brought many personal possessions with him from Austria. His German and English books, his Thai grammar and dictionary were all in place on the bookshelf, and all of Hans's clothing hung in a neat row in the closet. Jan and Snit knew what Hans had in the way of a wardrobe and knew that nothing was missing except a pair of shorts, a khaki shirt, and his sandals, which he obviously must have been wearing. When it came to the workroom, Mr. Grimes helped them with their inspection. The aluminum-foil rolls containing the geological maps were all in the cupboard, and all the instruments, rulers, cartons of ground models, and drawing tools were in their proper places. Nothing was missing, and there was nothing to suggest that any strangers had entered the barrack.

"Oh!" Snit suddenly cried. "The typewriter. It's gone!"

Snit was fascinated by the typewriter, which Hans had permitted him to use now and then. He had shown the boy how to handle the small portable machine, and Snit had eagerly begun to practice the art of typewriting. He was prouder over his typing skill than over his victories at ping-pong, and he had confessed to his friends that he was saving money to buy a typewriter with Thai characters on it.

"I don't understand it," Mr. Grimes said, shaking his head. "Here he goes and disappears with just his shirt, shorts, and sandals. He even left his keys on the table but took his typewriter. Why that, in particular, and nothing else?"

It was one more question no one could answer logically. About midday, Mr. Grundvahl called from the airport and, upon learning that Hans was still gone, promised to drive over to the police station at once and inform them of the dis-appearance.

At lunch, Mr. Grimes merely picked at the rice Snit had prepared and the corned beef he had warmed up to go with it. The boys' appetites were no better. Suddenly, Mr. Grimes slammed his fork down on the table and arose impulsively.

Turning to the boys, he said, "I'm going along to see the police, too. Your father is a fine man, Jan, a real gentleman. But in this case, I doubt if it will work to be a gentleman. We need someone who can pound his fist on the table. And an old well-digger like myself is much better suited to . . ."

Before the boys had time to reply, he was already outside the area. Naturally, the Freckles boys agreed with their father, and Jan, too, realized that a little arrogance at police headquarters might just help. Snit didn't say a word as he played with the rice on his plate.

"I have an idea," he said at last. "I'll go over to the residential area and ask the people there if anyone saw where Hans went yesterday."

Accompanied by Dog, he took off; half an hour later he came back with a discouraging report. No one had seen Hans all day. Soon Mr. Grimes returned, too, even angrier than he had been earlier.

"Protocol, protocol, empty promises," he growled sullenly as he saw the puzzled expressions on the boys' faces. "But I am going to see to it that they get him back. Not one more minute of drilling is going to take place here until he returns. . . . If they want any wells, they can darned well establish his whereabouts first!" Without waiting for a response, he turned to Snit.

"Run out to the drilling tower, Snit, and tell the workers

to stop everything. They don't need to bother to come here tomorrow, either. Ask how much we owe them in salary and give them a week's severance pay. There's some money in the little cashbox in the cupboard, and we can take their salaries out of that. I don't want the workers to suffer over this. Understand? And if anyone comes and complains that I took money out of the cashbox, I'll take responsibility myself for the entire sum."

The boys were aware that this was a big and important decision. If they stopped work and Hans didn't come back soon, no one would know whether the residents of Bangkok would ever have clean drinking water. They all knew that it was no easy matter to find hydraulic engineers and master drillers. For that matter, who would want to be a replacement, knowing that his predecessor had disappeared without a trace? These were the thoughts whirling through the boys' heads when Mr. Grimes told them of his decision.

"You just can't do that, Dad," Peter said at length. "This way you aren't hurting the people who have made off with Hans; you're hurting the local children. Think it over again before you send the workers away."

"There is some merit in your objection, son," Mr. Grimes said in an unusually calm voice. "But don't get it into your head that I've acted too hastily. In the first place, I can't assume the responsibility for drilling without Hans. If the drill tip were to break or if we were to hit water or if some accident happened on the job, I would have to answer for continuing the work without an engineer. But that's not the main objection, because I've never been afraid of responsibilities. The important thing is that if I suspend the work, we'll draw the attention of the Thai officials to Hans's dis-

appearance. Many things happen in this part of the world—
things that are merely forgotten without anyone's caring.
And I won't tolerate having Hans disappear and then be
forgotten."

Mr. Grimes walked over toward the drilling tower, and
Snit followed him obediently. Several minutes later the machinery was silenced, and the sudden quiet made the boys
more disheartened than before.

Chapter Nine

❖❖❖

A LETTER AND NOTHING MORE

If Mr. Grimes had really thought that Hans's disappearance would merely drown in a sea of papers at the police station, his suspicions were certainly not confirmed. On the afternoon of the work stoppage, the chief of police came to the site with three plain-clothes detectives and four policemen. The detectives and policemen examined everything thoroughly and questioned Snit for almost two hours. The chief also sent one detective and a policeman to the residential area to find out if anyone had seen the *farang* engineer on Sunday.

Mr. Grimes put it on record that, until further notice, he was forced to suspend operations, and he turned over some of the keys to the chief of police. The cupboards and the barrack were locked and sealed with the police signet. In accordance with Mr. Grimes's instructions, the machinery was covered with tarpaulins, and the chief gave orders for a twenty-four-hour guard at the approach to the site. These measures, in turn, meant that Snit's employment was at an end and that he would have to leave the site. Snit was deeply disturbed at being unemployed and homeless simultaneously, not so much for his own sake as for the fact that he feared he would lose his friends. But Mr. Grimes had already considered the matter. When the chief of police told Snit that he would have to leave the site, the master driller explained that the boy, in that event, would have to live at the hotel until they could find another place for him. Snit had no especially happy memories of the hotel with its impolite porter, and the expression on his face was not one of joy.

Jan, sensing how he felt, immediately stepped in and came to his rescue.

"Hey, can't Snit come and live with us instead?" he asked Mr. Grimes.

"Are you sure that your mother will have no objections?" Mr. Grimes asked.

"I'm positive that she'll be glad to have Snit for a while. She knows that he's one of my best friends," Jan answered with assurance.

And he was right, because Mrs. Grundvahl gave her son's friend a hearty welcome. There was lots of space in Jan's room, and it was easy to find him a place to sleep. But he refused to try a bed.

"I couldn't sleep on one of those things!" he explained apologetically. "I'd be scared that I'd fall off once I was asleep."

In line with the Thai custom, Mrs. Grundvahl put down a thick fiber rug in Jan's room and gave Snit a small hassock for his head and a blanket to cover him.

Mr. Grundvahl, too, was delighted to have Snit as a house guest, adding, in his practical manner, "Now you'll have lots

of time to talk to one another, Jan, and enough time to teach
Snit to read and write English, because it will come in very
handy for him as time goes by."

Despite all their friendly preparations, Snit had a hard
time sleeping that night. Not even the fact that his devoted
companion, Dog, was well cared for in the garden offered
him any solace.

The next morning Jan awakened at the sound of the slam-
ming of a car door. Looking at the clock, he found to
his great surprise that it was already nine—they had been up
late the previous evening and obviously he had overslept.
Snit's sleeping mat was already neatly rolled up in a corner,
and Snit himself was outside helping Chan the cook on the
veranda. Jan soon figured out that it was Mr. Grimes who
had slammed the car door. He was coming up the steps, followed by the Freckles boys. Mr. Grimes asked for Mr.
Grundvahl at once. As it happened, he was on the afternoon
shift at the airport and was spending the morning at home.

Jan dressed hurriedly and came down just as the family
was joined at the breakfast table by Mr. Grimes. The master
driller wasted no time with explanations but took a letter
out of his pocket and put it down in front of Mr. Grundvahl.

"This came in the mail today," he said as Mr. Grundvahl
picked up the envelope, took out the letter, and began reading aloud.

"Dear George,

"You must forgive me for leaving without talking with
you, but I was in a desperate hurry. All last week I was nego-
tiating with someone who offered me a job contract
in one of the neighboring countries. The job has to do with

drilling for oil, and the salary is more than twice as much as the World Health Organization pays me here. Naturally, I have to think of my own future, which is why I finally accepted their offer. And since I had to assume my duties immediately, I took off without saying good-by to anyone.

"I am truly sorry that our collaboration had to come to such an abrupt end, but I am sure that the World Health Organization will replace me very shortly with another engineer.

"I would be grateful if you could take care of my personal things, which I left at the site. As soon as I get matters squared away on my new job, I'll let you know where they should be sent.

"Give the Grundvahls my best greetings. I'm really sorry that I didn't have an opportunity to say good-by to any of you. I do send my best wishes for a successful conclusion to the project.

"Best, warmest greetings,

Hans Nittel"

For a few moments silence reigned, but finally Snit spoke up. "He didn't even tell Mr. Grimes to say hello to me," he said sorrowfully.

"Look, stupid," said Freckles the younger. "You don't think for a moment that he really wrote that letter himself, do you?"

"Well, who else could have written it?" Snit asked, but Freckles II had no chance to answer since Mr. Grimes himself had the floor again. It was Mr. Grundvahl's opinion he was interested in, not the boys' petty quarrels.

Mr. Grundvahl studied both the letter and the envelope for a while, saying finally, "The letter was mailed here in

Bangkok and postmarked on Sunday, the day Hans disappeared."

Jan asked to see the letter, and he, too, examined it carefully. Judging by its appearance, he thought it must have been written on Hans's typewriter. Jan had seen a good many things written on that machine, and he was pretty sure he was right. The handwriting looked like Hans's own—Jan was familiar with Hans's signature from the weekly reports they sent to the World Health Organization.

When Jan was through scanning the letter, Mr. Grimes said, "In connection with this, I think I ought to mention that about a week ago, I went down to the hotel bar one evening to have a drink, only to be accosted by a Malayan who spoke very good English. He introduced himself as the agent for a huge oil company, but I didn't really need to introduce myself because he knew exactly who I was. To make a long story short, this Malayan offered me a job contract with an astronomical salary and very good working conditions. When I informed him that I had other plans and was not interested, he countered by doubling the salary. At that point I became genuinely interested, since I began to wonder what kind of outfit this was that could pay such fantastic salaries. The Malayan explained that some geologists in Malaya had come upon unbelievably large oil deposits and that they were the richest deposits hitherto discovered. The company had begun digging in secret, but suddenly their master driller had gotten sick and was unable to continue working. When the Malayan realized that I was interested and thought I was taking it all seriously, he came out with what turned out to be the catch—the post would have to be occupied im-

mediately, with absolutely no delay. When I told him that
I had a contract with the World Health Organization, he
merely laughed and threw up his hands. 'Who cares about
them?' he said. 'Their pay is so bad that you have no reason
to be loyal to them.' I got mad at his implying that I would
even think of breaking a contract just on the grounds that
someone had offered me a higher salary, so I told him to
go."

"Do you mean that perhaps Hans got a similar offer from
the Malayan and accepted it?" Grundvahl asked.

"Hard to say. I've just known the boy for a couple of weeks,
and I don't really know what he's like. But I do know that
he is underpaid and at the beginning of his career, so maybe
he was tempted by the huge salary. People do strange things
when it comes to money."

"That just can't be so!" said Jan, almost beside himself. "I
know Hans inside and out, and I know that he's not
interested in making piles of money. He told me himself
that he took this job with the World Health Organization
because he felt he had a duty to contribute something to the
underdeveloped countries. That's why I don't believe a word
of that letter."

"We don't either!" cried the Freckles boys in chorus. "The
whole letter is nonsense. It's almost certainly one of Scarface's latest tricks."

Mr. Grimes had to silence his sons in order to be able to
continue.

"Well, I must admit that I didn't for a minute get the impression that Hans was particularly money-hungry. It does,
though, seem strange that he would just disappear and not

take his personal effects with him. If he really has gone to Malaya, he certainly would have needed his instruments, and they're still out at the site."

"One more thing," Mr. Grundvahl added. "If Hans really went to Malaya, he would have needed his passport. And that was out there among his other things in the cashbox, up to yesterday, anyway."

"So there! You are admitting yourselves that he can't have just gone away," Jan said triumphantly.

The two grownups were actually highly doubtful that the letter was genuine. But suddenly Mr. Grundvahl happened to think of something.

"It's no trouble for me to call the airport and find out if Hans was on the passenger list of any planes taking off for Malaya on Sunday," he said.

It turned out that no Hans Nittel was on any of the passenger lists for the planes that had departed on Sunday. With that, Jan and the other three boys felt that the matter was settled, but Mr. Grimes was not completely convinced. He pointed out that Hans could have traveled under an alias and that he didn't necessarily have to have left by plane. There were railway connections between Bangkok and Kuala Lumpur in Malaya, and you could get there by car, although, taking into account the condition of the roads in Thailand generally, you couldn't call it a pleasure trip.

Finally, Mr. Grundvahl and Mr. Grimes brought the discussion to a close by getting in the car and driving to the police station. The boys tried in vain to stop them from giving the letter to the police.

"They'll use it as an excuse to suspend all the investigations," Jan said in a worried tone, staunchly backed up by

the Freckles boys. Mr. Grundvahl quieted them by promising
that he and Mr. Grimes would point out to the chief of police that they had grave doubts about the authenticity of the
letter and that Hans didn't have his passport with him.

Once the men had taken off, the boys held a council of
war. They were completely agreed that Hans couldn't have
left his job of his own accord. The man from Malaya who
had tried to talk Mr. Grimes into leaving his job with the
artesian wells was almost surely a provocateur and nothing
more. Suddenly, Jan hit his forehead with his hand, walked
to the other end of the room, and got the telephone book.
For a short while he leafed through the pages until he found
what he was looking for.

"Embassy of the Federation of Malaya, Sathorn Tai Road
35," he read aloud.

Several minutes later they were on their way to the
Malayan Embassy—all four of them. There they were received by a polite clerk who told them that no one at the
embassy knew anything about any company that was concerned with digging for oil in Malaya. Neither did they have
any information on any agent from a Malayan company who
had come to Bangkok to recruit master drillers or engineers.
The clerk checked to see if anyone by the name of Hans Nittel had sought an entry permit for Malaya, but the answer
was again negative.

Out on the wide street, Sathorn Tai, it was Paul's turn to
come up with an idea.

"Hans is an Austrian citizen," he said. "Why don't we go
over to the Austrian Embassy and tell them what has happened. Somewhere I read that embassies always raise a ter-
rific fuss if any of their citizens disappear abroad."

The Austrian Embassy was at the other end of the city, on Rajavithi Road, near the royal palace, Chitra Lada. It wasn't very pleasant trudging through the heavy traffic and the masses of people who swarmed on the sidewalks in the oppressive heat, but finally the exhausted, perspiring boys arrived at the villa where the embassy was housed. The boys were received by a secretary of the embassy, an amiable, pleasant young man who, noticing how tired the boys were, ordered a glass of ice-cold orange juice for each of them.

When the secretary realized that the matter concerned Hans Nittel, he was more than interested. Hans was well known at the embassy, so the secretary listened attentively to the boys' story, hurrying then to talk to the ambassador. Through the half-open door, the boys could hear the ambassador calling the Thai Foreign Department and requesting the Thai authorities, in no uncertain terms, to institute any necessary measures immediately to assure the return of the missing Hans Nittel.

Before the daily rainstorm began, the boys had returned to the Grimeses' hotel, where Mr. and Mrs. Grimes had just sat down to lunch in the restaurant. Jan and Snit were invited to join the family, an invitation they eagerly accepted. The long walk had given them extraordinary appetites. While the boys waited for lunch to be served, they received a report on what Mr. Grimes and Mr. Grundvahl had accomplished at the police station. It wasn't much. The chief of police had noted that they didn't believe the letter to be authentic and had himself said that it seemed peculiar that Hans would just have gone off headlong. But, on the other hand, it seemed as if the signature were Hans's own. The chief had promised to continue the investigation.

When Mr. Grimes found out what the boys had been up to, he praised them for their efforts and said it had been a splendid idea to go to the embassies. He admitted, a little shamefacedly, that he had forgotten to consult some readily available information about oil companies in Malaya. He went to his room and brought down a small book called *The Oil Industry Yearbook,* explaining that it listed all important particulars and statistics on oil in general. But the book had nothing about drilling for oil under the heading "Malaya."

Later, Mr. and Mrs. Grundvahl joined them, and naturally all conversation centered on Hans.

"For the time being, there's nothing to do but wait," Mr. Grundvahl said. "But if Hans actually has gone to Malaya, he will let us hear from him, according to what was in the letter, within a few days, telling us where he wants his things sent. So if we don't get another letter soon, it may be further proof that this letter is a forgery."

Five days passed. Sunday came and went and a new week began, but still they hadn't received a second letter from Hans. The desk porter had grown accustomed to seeing the Grimes boys regularly, three times a day, immediately following the mail delivery. With each passing day, both the boys and their parents were more and more convinced that the letter in which Hans had told about his hurried journey was a forgery that simply couldn't have been written by him. Simultaneously, they began to be more and more worried about what could have happened to Hans. Mr. Grimes went to the American Embassy to tell them of his disappearance, but they naturally couldn't do anything for an Austrian citizen. He also wrote a long, detailed letter to the World

Health Organization, telling them that Engineer Hans Nittel had disappeared and that, consequently, the work had had to be suspended.

To judge by his appearance, Snit was the most worried of all. Jan devoted himself wholeheartedly to his friend, involving him in the mysteries of the English alphabet and teaching him all sorts of school subjects. Sometimes they went to the movies, and Mrs. Grundvahl did everything in her power to cheer up the nice young Thai boy. But Snit became gloomier and sadder and had seemingly lost all interest in what was going on around him. He began to go out for long walks with Dog, not returning until time to eat in the evening. He never mentioned what he had been up to the entire day, but sometimes both he and Dog seemed utterly worn out when they returned.

Early one morning when Snit and his dog were ready to go on one of their mysterious rambles, Jan made up his mind to follow them. Without letting Snit see him, he stayed behind about a hundred yards. When the boy and the dog got to a certain street corner, Snit took a piece of yellow cloth out of his pocket and let the dog smell it. Jan recognized the yellow rag immediately. It was a piece of the robe that the fake monk had had on when he tried to blow up the machinery. The dog smelled the rag carefully, after which he sniffed around a little with his nose pressed close to the ground. But obviously he found no scent which matched that of the cloth. Finally, as if to say that he was tired of the whole thing, he would suddenly lift his head and continue on.

Snit repeated his little ceremony with the rag about once every block, but each time with the same disheartening result. Soon they reached a wide, heavily trafficked street, Rajadamnoen Avenue, which, in spite of the early hour, was already in full swing. There sat Snit, crouched by the side of a building, while the dog went around smelling the legs of all the passers-by. They kept at it for a whole hour, and Jan, tired of just standing around, decided to go and join Snit. But at that moment, Dog threw himself out into the stream of traffic and rushed over to the other side. The street had a steady stream of cars, three-wheeled bicycles, and other vehicles, and Dog was in great danger of being run over. Snit arose, too, and rushed after his dog. A concert of horns and a stream of oaths arose before they had made it to the other side!

Dog headed straight to the south along the sidewalk, without bothering about the many pedestrians he almost knocked over. Snit scurried along about ten yards to the rear, trying hard to catch up. But his size made it harder for him to push his way through the crowds of people coming in both directions, and the distance between him and the excited dog grew and grew.

Jan realized that it was impossible to catch up with the fleet-footed Snit and his even faster dog, and finally he gave up. Instead, he remained standing on the sidewalk watching where they went. Clearly, the dog had found what he was looking for because he speeded up, yipping and barking. Soon he was just a few yards from a bearded man in a white turban and Western clothes, who seemed terrified of the excited animal. Before Dog could catch up to him, the man stepped into a car that was parked waiting for him, and the car took off with a great roar. For a moment, the dog stood looking at his vanishing quarry and then began to chase the car. At the first corner the car swerved sharply away from the main thoroughfare, and Dog went out of sight.

Snit kept trying to catch up with his dog, but he was at least thirty yards behind when Dog turned down the side street. The boy got to the corner, but there he halted, out of breath and exhausted. By the time Jan finally caught up with him, he had begun to breathe normally again. But

neither the car nor the dog were to be seen on the side street, and the only evidence of the point at which the vehicle and its pursuer had disappeared was a whirling cloud of dust.

"That was Scarface," Snit explained. "And now Dog won't be able to catch up with him. Too bad that cars have to be so much faster than dogs."

"What gives you the idea that it was Scarface, anyway?" Jan said in amazement. "That man was a Sikh, and Scarface is no Sikh. Furthermore, he doesn't have a beard, either."

"Remember," Snit said, "Scarface wasn't a monk or a customs official either. You could put on a turban if you wanted to, and he could have let his beard grow since he paid us a visit out at the installation. Come to think of it, maybe that isn't his own beard. He might have put on a false beard."

Jan realized that Snit might be right, but he still wondered what had given Snit the idea of trying to track down Scarface again.

"Well, you see, I figured that Scarface still had some kind of finger in the pie, and I decided that if we could get hold of the false monk, perhaps we could force him to tell us what he had done with Hans. When I was out with Dog four days ago, suddenly he got excited and began to sniff and bark. We happened to be on Rajadamnoen Avenue, and I had Dog on a leash, but I noticed that he was pulling with all his might in the direction of an open air café. I let him have his way, and he stood outside this café barking at the top of his lungs. Out on the terrace sat several foreigners, two Thai officers, and a bearded man with sunglasses on. I didn't recognize either the foreigners or the officers—or the bearded man, for that matter. But when the man with the beard caught sight of us, he immediately got to his feet and went inside. I tied Dog up at the railing and walked inside myself, but the man had simply disappeared. He had gone out through the back door of the café. I asked the waiter if he knew the identity of the bearded man, and he replied that the man had just begun to frequent the place a few days before and that he always placed his orders in perfect Thai.

"It struck me that the bearded man probably was Scarface. Obviously, he had let his beard grow or was wearing a false beard to hide his scar. Thailanders never wear beards. But

he couldn't change his scent, and for that reason Dog recognized him. That was when I made up my mind to keep an
eye out for him, and now for three days I've been on the alert
over there on the corner in the hope that he would pop up
again. I was dead certain that Dog would recognize him, and
as you saw for yourself, I was right."

"But what would you have done if Dog had managed to
catch him?" Jan asked.

"Right across from my observation post is a traffic policeman. I figured that if Dog managed to catch Scarface, I
would hurry over to the policeman and tell him that the man
was wanted by the police and should be taken to the station
immediately. But now everything has gone up in smoke, and
Scarface has gotten away."

Just as he said that, Dog slowly emerged from the side
street. His weary legs barely shuffled along, his nose was
almost down to the ground, and his tail was between his legs.

"Good boy, Dog," Snit said comfortingly as he petted his
faithful friend. "Good dog. You don't need to be ashamed of
the fact that the car went faster than you could. Anyway, you
did your very best . . ."

With some additional petting, Dog regained his compo-
sure. Wagging his tail wildly, he licked his master's hands,
after which he got on his hind legs and attempted to lick his
master's face. After Dog had calmed down, they decided to
start for home. The minute they had told their story to Mr.
Grundvahl, he went straight to the telephone and let the
chief of police know what the boys—or, rather, the dog—
had discovered—namely, that the false monk with the scar
was still around the city disguised as a Sikh. The chief of police remarked that the man had picked a pretty good dis-

guise because there were thousands of Sikhs in Bangkok, and
almost every single one of them, faithful to tradition, wore
beards and turbans. Unfortunately, he went on to say, the
police would be overstepping the bounds of the law if they
were to stop everyone with a beard to ascertain whether it
were real or not.

But apart from that, the chief of police congratulated the
dog for his achievements and sent his best greetings to this
excellent four-footed police aide. The congratulations not-
withstanding, the next morning Chan, on his way to the market in the early hours of the morning, found the dog in the
garden, unconscious and frothing at the mouth.

The frightened Chan woke up the entire Grundvahl family. Snit was not to be comforted. He sank to the ground beside the dog, took his head on his knee, and tried to bring
him to by whispering tender words in his ear. All the while
he cried so hard that his whole brown body shook. After a
time, he got to his knees, put his folded hands to his forehead,
and bowing deeply, prayed fervently to Buddha to save Dog's
life. He promised Buddha a huge bouquet of magnolias and
ten sticks of sandalwood incense if he would spare his friend.

Mr. Grundvahl acted in a more practical fashion. Quickly,
he got dressed, put the seemingly lifeless dog in the car, and
drove to the nearest veterinary. Snit wrung his hands and
wailed, and even Mrs. Grundvahl, Jan, and Chan were des-
olate as they waited for Mr. Grundvahl to return. Finally,
they heard the car pull up, whereupon they all rushed to the
gate to find out what had happened.

"Take it easy. Just take it easy," Mr. Grundvahl said. "The
doctor used a stomach pump on him and gave him several
heart injections." As he was speaking, he lifted the helpless

animal from the back seat. The minute Dog caught sight of
Snit, he made a weak attempt at wagging his tail.

"But what happened, anyway?" Snit asked uneasily.

"He had been poisoned. Someone must have thrown some
poisoned food through the fence."

It was three days before Dog could stand on his legs again. Snit regarded his recovery as the occasion for giving the dog a name of his own. After excited, lengthy discussions with Jan and the Freckles boys, he finally decided that Dog would be called "Mikki" from now on. The name is Thai and means a mixture of wise, wonderful, clever, and other flattering adjectives—a name so aristocratic that even princes are seldom allowed to use it unless they are almost without equal.

That very day Snit bought a huge bouquet of magnolias and ten sticks of fragrant incense by way of keeping his promise to Buddha. After lunch, Mr. Grundvahl drove him to the cloister near the installation so that he could place his gifts at the feet of one of the gilded statues.

After he had said his prayers, one of the monks told him he was to have an audience with the abbot. The latter, of course, knew about Hans's disappearance and about the project having been stopped until further notice. The elderly priest promised Snit that he would ask at every cloister in the country to see if anyone knew anything about Hans. There were no less than eight thousand cloisters in Thailand, and the number of monks with their gold robes and shaved heads came to well over a hundred thousand. An organization that covered the entire country was now in the picture, helping to find the vanished engineer.

Chapter Ten

❖❖❖❖

JOURNEY INTO THE UNKNOWN

Another week passed with nothing happening, and everyone began feeling more and more helpless. Mr. Grundvahl paid another visit to the chief of police, who put his cards on the table and said that no less than fifteen detectives were assigned to the task of finding Hans and Scarface—unfortunately, in vain to date. And Jan called at the Austrian Embassy, which had once more intervened by putting more pressure on the Thai Foreign Department. The Department had received a communication from the World Health Organization requesting that everything possible be done to find the vanished engineer and hoping for rapid results.

Mr. Grimes began to talk about returning to the United States, and the whole family might have flown home if Mrs. Grimes hadn't gotten sick. It was nothing dangerous—a light stomach infection—but the doctor advised the convalescent against taking the long plane trip for at least a week. Snit had already begun discussing the possibility of his finding a new job, since he didn't want to impose upon the Grundvahls forever.

Mr. Grundvahl, however, asked him to stay with them for

a while yet and suggested that he attend a technical school, after which Mr. Grundvahl could possibly get him a job at the airport. But the technical course was not to begin before October—a cooler time of year—and that was months away. Jan's education in a British private school was also to begin in October.

Because of Mikki's health, further attempts at tracking down the culprit were out of the question. In addition, the weather had worsened, and the daily rainstorms often lasted two or three hours, a sure sign that autumn was on the way. The constant, depressing rain plus the feeling that they couldn't do anything about Hans didn't improve the boys' moods.

One morning a young monk appeared at the gate to the Grundvahl garden. Snit hurried over to greet him with all the respect that the customs of the country demanded. The monk delivered a message from the abbot, which said that the inmates of a cloister in a village called Fung had taken in a sick foreigner whose description seemed to tally with Hans's.

The monk's information pulled the boys out of their despair and gave them renewed hope. The Freckles boys immediately telephoned their father at the hotel, and at lunchtime another council of war was held by the four boys and two men. The discussion centered around whether they should turn to the police or rely on their own initiative, and this time a compromise was decided upon, to the unbounded delight of the boys. The decision was made that they would inform the chief of police of the message from the abbot, but at the same time they would make a trip to Fung and take a look at the sick foreigner. All four boys were completely convinced that the ailing man could be none other than Hans.

A glance at a map showed that Fung was located in the north of Thailand between the cities of Chiang Mai and Lampang, in the midst of "The Paradise of the North." The Thailanders themselves refer thus to the district since the climate, thanks to its nearness to the mountains and the heavy forests, is kinder than in Bangkok and the southern part of the country. Up in the highest mountain ranges, it happens occasionally during the winter that the temperature falls a little below freezing and that the waters have a thin coating of ice.

After a lengthy discussion, they decided to appoint Mr. Grundvahl the leader of the expedition; all four boys were to go along. Snit was necessary as an interpreter, and the other three campaigned so vigorously to go that their fathers hadn't the heart to deny their requests.

There were daily flights between Chiang Mai, the second largest city in the country, and Bangkok, taking three hours' time. But they decided to take the train instead, since the boys would be able to see so much more of Thailand.

The train was already at the station when Mr. Grundvahl and the boys arrived, and the small locomotive was belching a cloud of smoke and a stream of sparks. To his great delight, Jan discovered that the train was powered by wood and not by coal. The Freckles boys regarded riding on a train powered by wood as a sort of primitive amusement, but Snit, who had never in his life ridden on a train, cared not a whit as to how the locomotive was propelled.

The chair cars and sleeping cars, on the other hand, were not very different from what the boys were used to. The main difference was that the train was chock-full of passengers who couldn't sit still for a single minute. The Thailanders, happy, friendly, and open, went from compartment to compartment becoming acquainted with their fellow travelers and holding conversations right and left. In the beginning, they avoided the foreigners, but when the other passengers discovered that the boys were not averse to talking and that they even spoke a little Thai, they began to come in a stream every bit as steadily as to any of the other compartments. The two Freckles boys were especially popular, mainly because of their freckles. Most of their fellow travelers had never seen people with freckles before.

The entire afternoon the train chugged along to the north following the big river, through a rather flat and tedious landscape with rice fields divided by irrigation canals. The only thing that really impressed the boys was the huge number of buffaloes. These enormous, lumpy black animals slowly and majestically wading through the fields livened up the entire scene. At times the farmers and their animals were working very close to the tracks, which gave the boys a good opportunity to see, at close range, the massive beasts with their curving horns and loose skins. Snit told them that the buffalo was the farmer's most faithful helper. The animal is unbelievably strong and can, with very little effort, pull a plow that digs deep into the mud. In addition, buffaloes can stand high temperatures, but they are so fond of water that the minute the farmer stops driving them, they assemble at the nearest watering hole. Snit went on to say that the buffaloes are so indispensable they are accorded a good deal of respect. Children meeting them on the village streets or out in the meadows always speak to them as if they were people, saying, "Good morning, uncle buffalo," or "Good evening,

aunt buffalo." It is possible that they curtsy more deeply to
the lady buffaloes because the thick, rich buffalo milk and
the cheeses made from it are the favorite dishes of the Thai
children.

Huge fans were in motion at the top of every compartment
in the train, and the windows were all open, but still the heat
seemed oppressive. Train trips in subtropical countries are
not among the most comfortable experiences in the world.
Fortunately, one thing after another happened to divert the
boys' attention from the heat.

For one thing, they made the acquaintance of a real prince. After the crowd of visitors to the compartment had begun to thin out, a little white-haired man wearing the uniform of the Thai Railways suddenly appeared. On his shoulder were three gold stripes, the sign that he was a station inspector. With much bowing, he introduced himself as Prince Pibuphaiwong, and the group bowed in return. Snit bowed unusually deeply; it was evident that he was quite honored with the visit.

In fairly decent English, the prince told them that he was the inspector at a station somewhere in the middle part of Thailand and that he was now on the way home, having taken care of some official errands in Bangkok. Mr. Grundvahl replied by saying that he and the boys were on the way to visit a sick friend in the village called Fung. Finally, the railroad prince, after much bowing from both parties, said good-by and returned to his own compartment.

Jan and the Freckles boys besieged Snit with questions as to whether the station inspector really was a prince and how, if this were true, he got to be a station inspector. Snit became a little confused, but Mr. Grundvahl undertook to explain the matter by telling the boys that, among other privileges, the kings of Thailand had the right to have a number of wives. King Mongkut, who had reigned about a hundred years ago and who was regarded as the founder of modern Thailand, had had no less than thirty-five wives. These wives had presented him with over a hundred children who were all, naturally, princes and princesses with royal blood. The king's numerous descendants, in turn, had children who were also princes and princesses, which meant that the number increased in an unbroken stream. But, except for their royal blood, many of these princes and princesses had inherited very little from their parents, and a good many royal descendants in Thailand were thus without private means and had to work for a living as did everyone else.

"The present ruler of the country, King Phumiphon Aduldet, is a modern sovereign in every respect, and he has only one wife," Mr. Grundvahl said in conclusion.

Presently, dusk began to fall, and before they had finished eating their evening meal in the diner, it was totally dark. The mood of the group had begun to be a little gloomy again, as they were talking about Hans. Paul, in a pessimistic mood, said gloomily that he didn't believe for a minute that Hans was still alive and that his enemies must have done away with him. None of the other boys raised any opposition to his statement, evidence of the fact that they had long suspected this to be the case but had not dared admit it to themselves. Mr. Grundvahl, on the other hand, rebutted firmly and hastily.

"Don't believe it for a minute, boys," he argued. "You know that the Thailanders are practicing Buddhists, who wouldn't think of taking the life of even an animal. Murder is a crime that almost never takes place in this country, and we'll just have to trust that the people who found it convenient to have him out of the way wouldn't go so far as to commit murder."

Mr. Grundvahl's speech had a calming effect upon them, and when they retired to the sleeping car that night, it was with the fervent hope that the next day would bring the solution to the riddle—in other words, that the person being cared for in the village cloister would turn out to be Hans and no one else.

The next morning the boys awoke to new and fascinating scenery. During the night the train had left the plains and was now on its way through the mountainous country in the north. The flat rice fields with their numerous irrigation canals had given way to softly rising slopes with groves of high bamboo thickets here and there. The gossamer green of the young plants and the yellowish color of the older trees stood out against the dark green background. The higher foothills and mountains that the train approached during the morning were covered with dense forests of tall trees. As they entered the mountainous region, the boys could see lush growths of bushes and vines growing among the tree trunks. It seemed almost unthinkable that either man or beast could make his way through this mass of vegetation.

Both Jan and the Freckles boys had read a good deal about tropical forests, about the dangerous, secret world of the jungle, but they had never seen this world with their own eyes. Snit, on the other hand, who had been raised in a jungle landscape, was completely at home in this green labyrinth. He told the other boys that the huge trees were teak, the timber of which was so unbelievably hard and tough that the woodsmen often broke both axes and saws when they tried to fell them. The price of teak was very high because of the fact that it was so difficult to work with and that there was such a demand for it.

About noon, the train, blowing its whistle wildly, pulled into the station at Chiang Mai. The streets were bordered with small bamboo cottages, and the road wasn't even cobblestoned. This was Chiang Mai, no more than a large village in spite of its more than fifty thousand inhabitants.

The hotel at which they stayed was simply furnished in the Thai manner, which meant that they had to sleep on mattresses laid out on mats instead of in beds. The tall, tapering, gilded pagodas of two Buddhist cloisters dominated the peaceful, idyllic view from their hotel room. When they went down to eat, they saw a good many men and women dressed, not in the half European costume common in Bangkok, but in variegated, richly embroidered robes of silk or cotton. Mainly, they were from the villages in the surrounding mountains, where civilization and foreign influences had not yet reached.

With the help of the hotel porter, they managed to hire a jeep and a driver who knew the way to Fung. The boys were eager to get going immediately, but the chauffeur explained that it would be foolish to start off in the hottest hours of the day. Actually, the streets were empty, the shops were closed, and peace and quiet reigned for two hours. The boys had no choice but to go to their rooms and rest for a while—which was actually quite agreeable after their long trip.

Once the siesta was over, the jeep took off from the main street and pushed its way in among the surrounding forest-covered mountains. It climbed higher and higher along the narrow road, and the air grew clearer and cooler. By chance, just as they rounded a curve, there at the edge of the road stood two gigantic elephants, calm and dignified, paying no attention whatsoever to the jeep and its passengers. The boys almost fell off their seats in surprise. The driver, on the other hand, was obviously used to such encounters. He didn't let this unexpected barrier excite him; he merely applied the brake gently and began to toot. The elephants gave no heed to the noise, but soon a half-naked man in a red headdress, carrying a long bamboo pole, appeared from the woods. The driver and the man greeted each other amiably and exchanged a few words about the weather and each other's well-being after which the man, with a few well-aimed shoves from the rear, drove the elephants out of the road so that traffic could move.

The driver wanted to continue the trip immediately, but the boys begged him to stop for a few minutes, and the whole group got out. In answer to Snit's inquiries, the chauffeur told them they were clearing the woods and that the two elephants, together with some other animals, were helping in the work. In the wooded area, the help of the elephants was essential. It would have been impossible to get tractors or other motor-driven vehicles across the rugged terrain, and manpower would have been insufficient to haul the heavy tree trunks out of the woods. At the command of their caretakers, the elephants, however, could easily lift the felled trees with their powerful trunks, after which they skillfully rolled them down the slope to the river. Any tree that got caught in the dense underbrush was set in motion again by a perfectly aimed push of an elephant's trunk.

Down at the riverbank two other elephants were at work. Standing halfway in the water, they dragged the teak trees down into the river, pushing them out into the middle until they were carried away by the current. The powerful animals, with their flabby, wrinkled hides, performed their tasks rhythmically and surely, and the caretakers very seldom needed to interfere with the work.

The foreman told them that the animals belonged to various owners. There were farmers who owned a small herd of eight or ten elephants, while others had only one. The owners

hired their animals out for a certain sum to woodsmen who were clearing the forests, construction crews, or flood control troops. Elephants are very intelligent animals who understand, after a few words and jabs from their caretakers, what they are supposed to do. These work elephants are all tame. During the working day, there is no need to worry about their running away, but at night it can happen that one of them will be overcome with wanderlust. The owners know their animals well and can tell exactly which ones have to be tied up overnight with heavy chains so that they won't wander onto the wrong paths.

The boys became so fascinated by the elephants that they forgot all about Hans and would have stayed there for hours if Mr. Grundvahl hadn't reminded them that they had not come on this journey just to study elephants. Returning to the jeep, they started out again on the road that soon began to slope downward. Finally, they reached a cultivated valley, in the middle of which was a brook, resembling a band of silver in the sunshine. At the edge of the brook stood a long row of small bamboo cottages on poles. They had arrived at the village Fung, their destination.

The cloister was about a fifteen-minute walk from the village, and it looked very ancient. The quarters of the monks were surrounded by high stone walls, which, here and there, were broken by slender turrets. The highest turret of all, painted a light red, was right in the middle of the circle of buildings.

They parked the jeep in the village since, according to the driver, it would have been a terrible breach of etiquette not to walk the last lap to the cloister on their own feet. Snit agreed by saying that even very distinguished persons—up to and including the king—always arrived at the temple on foot to show their respect for Buddha and his servants. The minute the group climbed down from the jeep, they were surrounded by a mob of children. Soon even the grownups joined in the reception, and in no time the entire population of the village was gathered around the jeep. The driver did his best to keep the people away from the vehicle, but with very little success.

After a time, an elderly man came forward, introduced himself as the headman of the village, and invited the strangers to be his guests in his home. Snit tried to explain to him that they had urgent business at the cloister, but the man turned a deaf ear. Finally, they realized that they couldn't refuse to call on the man for a few minutes and drink a small cup of green tea with him. The headman and his family stared unashamedly at Mr. Grundvahl and the three white boys the entire time, making it quite clear what fascinated them so tremendously: their blue eyes.

"Certainly, we have seen other *farangs* here before," the headman explained to Snit and the driver, "but none of them has ever had such strange light eyes. Never could I have imagined that there were people this peculiar."

The headman's wife joined in the conversation as she asked Snit, "Can the strangers see just as well with their sky-colored eyes as we can with our genuine ones?"

When Snit answered in the affirmative, the old lady shook her head. "Strange. Very peculiar," she said. "I could never have imagined it was true."

After the teacups were emptied, the headman, with the driver as an intermediary, asked the group to be seated outside his house for a few minutes so that the other inhabitants of the village could have a chance to admire their strange blue eyes. Obediently, they sat on a little bench near the street, while the villagers marched past in parade. A few of them actually stopped for a moment to look the *farangs* in the eye at close range, and a small child even wanted to stick its finger in Jan's eye. Mr. Grundvahl and the boys were half amused, half irritated at being put on display in this fashion, but they endured their fate patiently.

Finally, the parade came to an end, and the headman gave them a small Buddha statue of teak and handed each a small bouquet as a sign of the village's esteem. It was impossible to be annoyed by these friendly, smiling people.

The gate of the cloister was guarded by two carved six-foot-tall warriors with dark green cheeks, a couple of sharp fangs on either side of their mouths, elegant gilded helmets, and red and green costumes. Both of these old statues were thrusting silvery curved sabers toward the visitors in order to keep all evil spirits from this building, which was en-shrined to Buddha. At Snit's request, the monk on guard at the gate informed the abbot of the arrival of the visitors, and he received them very warmly. After they had placed the bouquets given to them by the villagers at the foot of a ten-foot-high, gilded and reclining statue of Buddha, the abbot led them directly to the ailing *farang*. On a raffia mat inside a cool, pleasant building lay a man covered with blankets, with about a week's growth of beard. His whole body shook with chills and fever, and his pale lips were twitching.

"Malaria, obviously," Mr. Grundvahl declared.

But alas—the man who lay there shivering was nothing at all like Hans. After a time when the attack had subsided, the stranger was able to sit up, and a young monk gave him some tea and a white pill.

"Jean Bondy," the sick man said, introducing himself. "I am a French ornithologist. I've come here to northern Thailand to take a look at the bird life, since very few ornithologists have been here before. To my misfortune, I contracted malaria from the mosquitoes down in the jungle and was forced to find my way to the cloister. Lucky for me, I had a good supply of quinine with me and was able to tell the monks to give me a proper dose every time I had an attack of malaria. Over and above this, these good monks have provided me with all the comforts of life in their kindly way. I've been here for a week already, but I think the disease is losing its grip and that I'll be able to return to Bangkok soon. There I have in mind to enter a hospital and get cured of this horrible disease once and for all."

That was about all the French bird researcher managed to say between his rattling teeth before sleep overcame him after his violent attack of fever. He did thank them for their visit and assured them that he didn't need anything for the moment.

The boys were deeply disappointed when they left the cloister, and Mr. Grundvahl was not in a very good mood, either. The long trip had been in vain, and Hans was still missing. The return trip from Chiang Mai to Bangkok seemed endless, and they talked very little among themselves the whole time. Exhausted from the heat and stiff from their long journey by train, they arrived at home two days later, dispirited and downcast.

Chapter Eleven

❖❖❖

A SURPRISE AND A VISIT

From the station they took a taxi directly to the hotel, where the Grimeses lived. They found Mr. Grimes eagerly awaiting them. They scarcely had time to wash off the dirt of the journey before the master driller astonished them with his big news.

"Scarface has been caught! The police got him yesterday, and I have been down to identify him."

The boys were overjoyed, but Mr. Grundvahl was his usual calm self.

"Did he confess what he has done with Hans?" he asked.

"The guy is as tight as a clam and maintains that he knows nothing at all about Hans's disappearance," Mr. Grimes answered.

"But can't the police make him talk?" Jan said in irritation.

"No. I was there when the police questioned him, but he said repeatedly that he didn't have anything to say. He admitted that he was the one who had agitated the people to break in at the installation and that he had tried to blow up the drilling tower. But when the police chief asked about his motive, he just said that he hated *farangs* and wanted to stop them from spoiling the people of Thailand."

"Do you think he could possibly be a member of some political organization or some fanatic outfit?" Mr. Grundvahl asked.

"The police hit on that idea, but up to now they can't find any proof to back it up," Mr. Grimes said. "Naturally, this doesn't eliminate the possibility that he could have been acting in accordance with orders from some misguided sect. Against that, though, is the fact that he had plenty of money on him when they caught up with him."

Mr. Grimes went on to tell them that, as Scarface was a former police lieutenant, the detectives knew him by sight. The chief had figured out that the man would certainly try to get away from the city once he knew he had been discovered. Accordingly, the detectives guarded railway stations, airports, and all roads leading from Bangkok. All automobiles driving along the country roads were stopped and not allowed to continue until every passenger had identified himself, and a detective was assigned to a window at the railway station so that he could get a look at every single person who bought a ticket.

On the third day after this intensive check began, a policeman on a country road to the south tried to stop a taxi, but the driver didn't obey him and speeded up instead. The driver in question had a beard and dark glasses, which in itself was rather suspicious, since every taxi driver in Bangkok is clean-shaven. The policeman had a powerful Harley Davidson motorcycle, and it took him only a few minutes to overtake the taxi and force it to a halt. Sure enough, the driver was Scarface, who had equipped himself with a thin beard after having so hurriedly left both his office and his house.

In addition, Mr. Grimes told them that the chief of police had requested the boys to come to police headquarters as quickly as possible for a confrontation with the criminal. The boys went straight down there, curious to see this arch enemy who had been captured alive. The chief had Scarface brought in, who was by this time clean-shaven. There wasn't the slightest doubt that this small, sullen man sitting before them was the same person—the robed monk from the installation.

"What have you done with our friend?" Snit asked.

Nothing about the expressionless face changed, and Scarface's answer was merely a shrug of the shoulders. Shortly thereafter, he was taken back to his cell, and the police chief told Mr. Grimes and the boys that, in spite of repeated questionings, they had gotten nothing of value from him. Jan was just about to ask why they hadn't, in that case, tried to improve his power of speech with a few cuffs on the ear, but he stopped himself in time, remembering how disturbed he always got when he read a newspaper account of the way in which some policeman mishandled apprehended criminals. Such things came under the heading of "police brutality," and Jan thanked his lucky stars that his brain, for once, was quicker than his mouth.

When they were about to leave, the chief expressed the hope that the riddle of Hans's disappearance would soon be solved, especially now that Scarface was in jail.

"I'm sure he'll change his mind after he has sat in his cell for a while," he added, but it sounded as if he really didn't believe his own statement.

"Well, we still haven't accomplished much of anything,"

Mr. Grimes said in disgust as they reached the street. "One good thing, anyway, and that is that Scarface didn't manage to escape the wheels of justice. He'll probably get a good prison term for all his crimes—the misdirection of the packing case, the riot out at the installation, and the other mischief he was behind."

"I don't see that it makes any difference if the man is hanged or elevated to the rank of prince, as long as we don't have Hans back!" one of the Freckles boys said bitterly.

The following morning as the Grundvahls sat at breakfast on the terrace, Chan appeared, announcing a visitor. It was the same elegant Chinese who, some time earlier, had introduced himself as Fu Man-Tsu's secretary and had delivered his present. On this occasion he had with him a little roll of parchment tied with gold braid, which he handed over with a respectful bow—but not to Mr. Grundvahl—to Jan.

"The respectful author of these lines, the simple, unworthy, old Fu Man-Tsu, would regard it as a mark of distinction if the richly endowed, promising Mr. Grundvahl, Junior, would grant his request of an honored visit. May the sun of fortune shine constantly upon Mr. Grundvahl, Junior, and upon all the other members of his honorable family."

This was the text printed with red India ink in graceful letters on the parchment, which Jan now passed to his father. Mr. Grundvahl asked the secretary to be seated, but he smilingly refused the offer.

"When does Mr. Fu Man-Tsu want me to visit him?" Jan inquired.

"If it suits young Mr. Grundvahl, my master would be glad if this visit could occur immediately," the secretary answered.

"My master, Fu Man-Tsu, has sent his personal car to fetch his eagerly awaited guest. He would like to discuss a very important matter of great concern to Mr. Grundvahl, Junior," he explained.

As a matter of fact, the automobile stood outside the gate, with the golden dragons on the sides and the chauffeur in gray livery at the wheel. The minute the chauffeur caught sight of the secretary accompanied by Jan, he scurried out of the car, opened the door, removed his cap, and bowed deeply. The secretary sat beside the chauffeur, and Jan felt very much alone and lost in the back seat.

"What a commotion over the fact that I saved a little boy from drowning," he thought to himself. "If the fellows back home in Sweden could see me now, they'd probably laugh themselves to death."

The decorated Chevrolet made its way through the city, continued northward, and finally arrived at the riverbank. From the main road a small, well-cared-for side road led down to the bank and, via a small stone bridge, over to a small island. The stone bridge was built in classic Chinese style, with two dark blue earthenware open-mouthed lions at the abutment. A Chinese in a blue silk garment quickly opened the gilded gate at the bridge, and the car rolled along through a tree-lined avenue up to a villa of white marble. Scarcely had it come to a stop before the wrought-iron gates were opened, and Fu Man-Tsu himself received them. The elderly Chinese bowed politely to Jan, letting him lead the way into the villa—or, rather, palace.

Jan had been in the palace in Stockholm, and a couple of times at the opera, not to mention all the luxury homes he had seen in technicolor movies. But never had he dreamed that he would see anything like Fu Man-Tsu's "simple" home. The corridors were carpeted in light blue rugs with various animal figures woven by a master craftsman. Along the walls were rows of columns decorated with lovely red lacquer work.

The walls were painted with black lacquer, and the shiny surfaces had been embellished by some Chinese artist's hand —dragons, imaginative flowers, and landscapes, all in glistening gold. The three enormous windows were framed by heavy draperies in black, red, and gold, and the windowpanes were thin pieces of jade. These leaf-thin panels were adorned with semiprecious stones, and the sunlight coming through had a greenish cast.

Fu Man-Tsu led his guest to a side door with splendid bronze plaques. The room, however, to Jan's great surprise, was almost puritanical in its simplicity. Off-white walls, a simple desk, a bookcase, and two chairs constituted the entire furnishings.

"This is my private workroom," Fu Man-Tsu explained. "The pomp and elegance are for the sake of outsiders, but I usually like to receive my friends in here. And it would please me very much if I could regard you as my friend."

Jan was aware of the elderly man's simple grayish white robe and of his speech, so free from Oriental accent. Fu Man-Tsu's speech was perfect Oxford, clipped English. He motioned to Jan to sit down, and immediately thereafter a Chinese servant came in with a tray and placed a lovely, thin porcelain bowl containing candied ginger and a little cup of tea before Jan.

"I hope you don't think for a moment that I have forgotten you or that I feel that I have repaid my debt of gratitude to you with the modest trifle I sent when you saved little Ho-Chin. You saved the life of my great-grandson, and there is no way in the world of repaying such a debt. But since that time, I have kept up with what was happening to you and your family here in Bangkok, and I have also received some information about you from Sweden. Unfortunately, my knowledge of Swedish is so scanty that I am unable to converse in your beautiful language," said the elderly man—the latter two sentences in Swedish. "But I hope that you'll understand just as well if I speak English," he added.

Jan was utterly astonished that the elderly Chinese even understood Swedish. "What an amazing man," he thought to himself.

"May I ask how your little great-grandson is?" he inquired.

"Little Ho-Chin is very well and is making splendid progress. I would be overjoyed if you would accompany me some time and pay a visit to the boy. But now, my young friend, you must let me tell you the real reason I have asked you to come here. As I mentioned, I have tried to follow your comings and goings here in Bangkok, and I am glad to say that I know you are in good company and doing a very important job. Therefore, I realized immediately what a blow it must have been to you to lose your friend."

"Oh, then you know about Hans's disappearance," Jan said.

"Naturally. I have knowledge of most things that happen in Bangkok and the surrounding territory," Fu Man-Tsu explained with a knowing smile. "A man with my extensive business interests has to keep well informed."

"Well, then, if you are that well informed, perhaps you know what is behind Hans's disappearance," Jan continued.

"I do, indeed. But first let me pose a few questions to you. Have you tried to figure out who might be interested in having Engineer Nittel disappear, which, in turn, would throw the drilling off schedule?"

"We've all puzzled over that matter and discussed it, but we haven't managed to come up with a thing. Hans doesn't have an enemy in the world . . ." Jan said hesitantly. "Naturally, we realize that it must be someone who wants to sabotage the drilling. But why anyone would want to do that is more than we can figure out."

"It's easy to see that neither you, your father, nor Mr. Grimes are businessmen," Fu Man-Tsu replied. "I'm sure you think I sound cynical, but a long life of experience has taught me a great deal. Money and materialistic interests rule the world, at least here in Asia. In this case, it's simply that a well-known economic investment is threatened by a project to give the people of Bangkok free drinking water. So this certain person, in his own special way, is trying to see that the well-drilling is stopped altogether. Tell me, young man, what kind of water do you use in preparing food at home, and what do you usually drink?"

"Every morning a delivery truck comes with fresh water, and Chan—he's our cook—buys four pails of water for the preparing of food. I guess the truck gets water from some well in the area. With our food we drink soda or some sort of soft drink, and Father has a bottle of beer with his dinner."

"Well, I suspect you're beginning to understand what I mean," said Fu Man-Tsu. "Especially if I tell you that these wells, the delivery trucks that come with the water, the factories that make the soda and soft drinks, and all of Bangkok's breweries are owned by one and the same person. If there were to be free drinking water for the populace, the purchase of water from the delivery trucks and the consumption of soft drinks and beer would go down appreciably. You see what I mean."

"Yes, I do. Then Hans is the victim of someone who puts his economic interest above all else. And it must have been the same person who redirected the shipment of the sixth case down at the harbor, who sent out the men who stole the motorboat, and who arranged for someone to incite the people in the area. But pure water would save thousands of children and grownups from various sicknesses. I can't imagine that there are people who think their economic interests are more important than the welfare of the people in general," Jan said.

"Alas, there are many such people. There's an abundance of them especially in countries where for thousands of years no one has given any consideration to the lives and rights of others—just their own interests. In the vicinity of the jungle, the law of the jungle prevails," Fu Man-Tsu said.

"May I ask you one more question?" Jan said, and the elderly man nodded.

"Well," he continued, "then Scarface—that's what we call the former police lieutenant—is under the thumb of this man you're talking about. But how could a policeman in a position of responsibility get himself mixed up in a mess like this?"

"Well, to begin with, Scarface, as you call him, became an opium smoker many years ago. Not very many Thailanders are slaves to that habit, since the addiction is mainly among the Chinese living in this country. But in any event, the police lieutenant became a hopeless addict, and in no time it became more and more expensive for him to

get enough of the drug to satisfy his craving. The salary of a
police lieutenant doesn't stretch very far, and fairly soon it
happened. Someone came along and offered him some
money. In exchange, the man asked only for a 'few small
favors' now and then—things that the lieutenant had no
trouble arranging in his position. There were no big matters
at all, but things that were on the shady side of the law. We
call this sort of thing corruption, the curse of the underdeveloped countries. By the time the dealer began to ask for
bigger and bigger favors, the police lieutenant was already
in his clutches, unable to deny the favors for fear he would
reveal his earlier, smaller mistakes. Actually, it was a matter
of blackmail."

"Now I'm beginning to understand," Jan said. "Scarface
has clammed up with the police because he doesn't dare reveal his leader. He's afraid he'll be worse off if he tells everything he knows. Am I right?"

"Precisely," Fu Man-Tsu said, nodding. "And let me
point out one other thing in this connection. The businessman who has caused you so much trouble is a very influential
person. His family is one of the most aristocratic in the country; he's a multimillionaire, and he has many friends in high
posts. An accusation against him would cause you yourself,
to say nothing of your father, some very serious trouble . . ."

"But the man is a criminal and an extortionist who . . ."
Jan interrupted.

"Control yourself, my friend. I know perfectly well how
you feel, but don't forget for a moment that you have absolutely no proof about the man. I've told you all this, but you
must regard the information as confidential, friend to friend.
And I must ask you to give me your word of honor that you

will not reveal the source of your information. I have no desire to have a falling out with this man, especially since he has good friends in very influential positions. I am too old for this sort of intrigue; I'm a businessman and not a crusader."

"I promise," Jan answered, his spirits somewhat crushed. "But will you allow me to share this information with my father and Mr. Grimes?"

"Of course. A son should never keep anything secret from his father. That is one of the basic rules of Chinese etiquette, and the doctrine of our great philosopher, Emperor Fu-Tse, almost three thousand years old, has much wisdom in it. Mr. Grimes is your friend, and the friends of my friends must, in turn, be my own friends. That, too, is part of the Emperor's doctrine."

Shortly thereafter, the Chevrolet with the magnificent gold dragons drove Jan back to his home. Snit and the Grimes boys, who had arrived for a visit in the meantime, were eagerly awaiting his return, since they were quite sure that Jan's visit to the elderly Chinese gentleman had something to do with the mystery of Hans's disappearance.

The Freckles boys, and Mr. Grimes as well, gave way to righteous indignation.

"All the Western nations, and especially the United States, have gone and collected tax funds and voluntary contributions from their citizens just to help the underdeveloped countries," Mr. Grimes said bitterly. "Generous, friendly people have given millions of dollars for such purposes. And then come the gangsters and greedy speculators, trying to keep the poor and needy from their share of the benefits. The very least I can do is go to our ambassador and tell him to send a report to Washington so that we can put an end to all this intrigue."

"Not so fast, my friend," Mr. Grundvahl said calmly. "This is nothing new. Both your ambassador and your government know perfectly well that certain individuals or even foreign governments often try to hinder, or exploit, beneficial projects. It will come as no surprise to them who work with the problems of the underdeveloped countries that corruption exists in Asia. And in addition, there is often racial prejudice and hatred for the white man. All these factors have to be taken into account, but you still have to do your best to overcome all the obstacles. Your government is powerless to do anything about this. We'll have to try some other tactic."

Finally, Mr. Grimes calmed down as he realized the logic of Mr. Grundvahl's argument. However, he was unshaken in his conviction that they had to do something fast and effectively and that Hans would have to be freed at any cost. How this was all going to be brought about, none of them could say. But on one point they were in complete agreement: they would gain nothing by going to the police with this new information. They had nothing but allegations and vague accusations to present—no real proof. And they all realized that the chief of police could hardly instigate any legal procedures against a multimillionaire with excellent connections in high places when he had only unverified details to go on.

Jan, however, was secretly hatching a daring plan of his own. The next morning, he dressed in his best clothes and rode his bicycle into the center of the city. He went straight to the modern office building where the administration headquarters of the brewery outfit was located. He had found the address in the telephone book. When he arrived, he told the guard on duty that he wanted to speak with the big boss. When asked by the guard if he had an appointment, he answered in the affirmative, whereupon he was sent up to the second floor.

Jan had been mistaken in thinking that a mere fib to the guard would gain him admittance to the big boss. He got as far as the waiting room, where he was met by a muscular and quite unfriendly watchman. He muttered something about an appointment, and Jan, blue-eyed and grinning, said, "Oh yes, the manager is expecting me."

At that point, still another door opened, and he was motioned in by a friendly, smiling secretary in European dress. Jan realized that any talk about an appointment would be useless here, so he tried a new strategy. He explained that he had a very important personal message for the big boss, only to be told that if he would write out the message, the secretary himself would see to it that it got delivered to the high official in question. Jan refused to give up, stubbornly and loudly demanding to see the boss himself. He was fully prepared for the fact that the secretary might simply throw him out, but his fears were groundless. His vitality apparently had made an impression on the secretary, who hesitantly reached for the intercom telephone.

"Now what!" Jan said impatiently. "Let's have a little action. I'm not used to being kept waiting this way."

And this was his big psychological mistake. Immediately, the secretary withdrew his hand from the telephone, answering in an agitated, shrill voice, "Are you threatening me? I'll show you a thing or two. Do you think you own the place?"

Jan's visit assuredly would have come to a sorry end if, a moment later, the door to the boss's office hadn't opened. A jovial, round-faced man stuck his head out to see what was causing all the commotion around his office. After an excited exchange of words on both sides, the manager, smiling, led Jan into his large office, which looked exactly as a manager's office ought to. Once in the room, he amiably asked Jan to have a seat.

"Well, well," he began genially. "Young Mr. Grundvahl wants to talk to me, if I'm not mistaken. You're the son of Flight Engineer Grundvahl, aren't you? In addition, I seem to recall that you are serving as a drafting assistant out at the drilling installation. Really a shame that the project had to come to a stop when the director skipped out. But now, to what do I owe the pleasure of your visit?"

Jan was aghast at the insolence of the man, but at the same time, he was surprised at how well informed he was about him since he—Jan—was entirely insignificant. For that reason, it took him a while to find the right words, and while he sat there formulating his introductory remarks, he decided that this man opposite him in no way resembled a big-time criminal, with his careful grooming, his gold-rimmed spectacles, his smiling countenance, and his sophisticated appearance. The puzzled expression on his round face reminded Jan of a goodhearted philanthropist more than a hard-bitten, greedy businessman. Nonetheless, Jan pulled himself together and immediately came forth with his trump card—the idea that he had secretly called "Operation Smartness."

"I have come here to suggest a point of agreement. You would surely prefer a compromise to utter defeat. And our suggestion is this: if you will immediately release Engineer Nittel and promise in the future not to cause any hindrance to his work, we'll promise not to instigate any legal measures against you."

The manager might throw him out at once or he might shower him with abuse. Jan had already figured out what he would do in either of these cases. But all that happened was that the man reached for his cigar box, chose an aromatic cigar, clipped off the end, and lighted it with his gold lighter. Blowing some perfect smoke rings, he then answered calmly and assuredly.

"Young man, your suggestion is highly interesting and worth a good deal of consideration. But unfortunately, it is not within my power to accept it. I am unable to release Engineer Nittel since I am not holding him prisoner anywhere. To be quite truthful, I haven't the slightest idea where Engineer Nittel is keeping himself these days."

"You're lying, and you know it," Jan said, trying to be equally calm and assured. "You know perfectly well who is holding my friend prisoner and where he is being held. Your underling—the former police lieutenant—has admitted everything. Don't waste time trying to laugh the whole matter off."

Jan's statement was an out and out bluff, since Scarface hadn't admitted anything at all, but it hit the man like a bomb. The smile on the man's face disappeared, and as he placed his cigar in a marble ashtray, he pressed a button. The secretary rushed in, and the manager said something in such a low voice that Jan couldn't understand a single word. Nodding, the secretary hurried out as fast as he had hurried in.

"That shot certainly hit its mark," Jan thought to himself.

"The manager was obviously interested in not having Scar-face do a lot of talking. But it was silly of him to show his cards so obviously. I thought he would be a more difficult person to catch."

"You're playing a pretty wild game, young man," the manager then said coolly. "And you're acting in a very foolish manner. Apparently you don't realize what a dangerous situation you're letting yourself in for. Have you considered the fact that it's very possible your good friend Engineer Nittel has defected to the neighboring Communist nation of North Viet Nam and has accepted a position there? How can you be certain that Engineer Nittel hasn't been a secret member of the Communist party all this time? We are struggling valiantly against Communism in this country—against fellow travelers and anyone who helps them in their dirty work. It's very seldom that such people have any great future among us."

"Don't waste your time," Jan remarked. "That ruse is as old as the hills. Anyone who stands in the way of your business interests is a Communist, and that's the end of that. But your suggestion doesn't go down with me at all. Hans Nittel has never been a Communist, and he would never dream of deserting his job and defecting to a Communist country. Hans came here to help your people and nothing else, and it's his help that you have tried to stop. And if you aren't already aware, I can tell you that the diplomatic circles here in Bangkok are all informed of the situation and are following the developments with great interest. As far as your threat to me personally goes, I couldn't care less."

With that he arose and pounded his fist on the table—just as he had seen Marlon Brando do in a television movie a while back—saying, slowly and clearly, "If Hans Nittel isn't back within twenty-four hours, we're going to take action against you. Do you get the picture? I have all the proof I need right in my hands."

Without waiting for the surprised manager's reply, Jan slowly walked out of the room. Passing both the secretary and the surly doorman, he was soon on the street again. As he rounded the corner and got on his bicycle, his knees began to shake, and perspiration began to drip from his forehead.

Chapter Twelve

❖❖❖

THE DRILLING MACHINERY RUNS AGAIN

Though it was still morning, it was oppressively hot. Jan sat in his room with the blinds drawn. While eating break- fast, he was looking at the English language newspaper pub- lished in Bangkok—a paper eagerly sought after by Thai- land's foreign colony and those who came to Thailand as tourists, but he wasn't paying much attention to what the paper had to say. Almost every waking moment since Hans's disappearance, Jan's thoughts had focused on little else. He half hoped that when the mailman came, there would be some word from or about his friend. Today the letter carrier was late, as was often the case, and Jan merely thumbed through the paper.

On the last page a list appeared each day of the travelers who had arrived in Bangkok. It gave the name, business, and homeland of the tourist, as well as the hotel he was staying in in the Thailand capital. This was the favorite feature of the newspaper for the whole Grundvahl family. Mama, Papa, and Jan were equally curious each day to find out if any acquaint- ances from Sweden had arrived. Although the Grundvahls were very much at home in Bangkok, they were occasionally homesick for the old country and especially for the friends they had left behind.

Jan read through the many American, English, and Japanese names, plus a few Indian and French ones thrown in. Suddenly, his eyes lit on the name Lars Hammar. It was well known. So, for that matter, was the man. He was a famous reporter who often wrote on world affairs and foreign countries for the *Swedish Daily Journal*, a Scandinavian newspaper to which the Grundvahl family had subscribed for many years. He was listed here as a reporter from Stockholm.

Jan, deep in thought, let the newspaper fall to the floor. His brain began to function at top speed.

No more than five minutes later Jan was on his bicycle pedaling as fast as his legs could go, heading toward the Hotel Esplanade, where, according to the paper, the reporter was staying. The hotel porter informed Jan politely that Mr. Hammar was sitting on the inside terrace just at the edge of the swimming pool and that he had just ordered a continental breakfast for himself. Several of the hotel guests were eating on the shaded terrace, but Jan had no difficulty in locating the person he was seeking. The reporter was wearing a plaid beach robe, and his hair was still wet from his morning dip. Engrossed in the morning paper, he sat waiting for his coffee. He was a good bit older than Jan had anticipated, with graying hair, and the wrinkles on his face resembled the pattern of rivers on a map. But he had an intelligent face, and he inspired confidence.

Jan walked straight toward him and tried to get his attention by clearing his throat. His strategy worked. The man in the beach robe lowered his paper and glanced up at the boy in front of him who, as good manners would demand, bowed and introduced himself.

"My name is Jan Grundvahl, and I'm a student from Lidingö. I wonder if you'd mind if I took a few minutes of your time?"

The reporter seemed both surprised and pleased at the idea of running into a fellow countryman in a hotel in Bangkok. Raising himself slightly from the chair, he reached out his hand, repeated his already familiar name, and motioned to Jan to sit in the chair on the opposite side of the small round table. Jan settled down and immediately began to speak, using carefully chosen words as one does when something very important happens.

After explaining his own presence in Bangkok, he immediately launched into the story of the hydraulic project and the subsequent disappearance of Hans Nittel. The reporter, clearly interested, asked a question now and then. Jan finished his tale with a brief account of his conversation with the manager of the brewery two days previously. Once he had finished, he remained silent for a moment, but the reporter realized that the boy had not tracked him down merely to tell his story. Shortly, Jan began to say what was really on his mind.

"I've told you all this because I think you might be able to help us. The twenty-four-hour deadline I gave the brewery manager is long since past, but Hans has not reappeared. I suspect the man found out that I was bluffing and has decided to do nothing whatsoever. Who knows? Maybe I've done Hans some harm instead of helping him, because now that man is naturally going to do everything in his power to make Hans disappear once and for all—perhaps by smuggling him over to North Viet Nam."

"You might be right," the reporter said, deep in thought.

"Well, that's why I'm asking for your help. A journalist like you has many more possibilities to poke around in something like this than other people do. I'm sure you would consider it important to see that an innocent person is released, that the Thailanders get free, pure drinking water, and that the water supply here is not controlled by a gangster!"

Jan's story caught the interest and concern of Mr. Hammar, but the reporter failed to see how it all hung together. To be sure, if a large Swedish newspaper were to give the story wide coverage, the other foreign correspondents in Stockholm would naturally report it to their own publications, and soon the story would hit the press all over the world. At that point, the Thailand officials would be forced to take action against the man who was behind Hans's disappearance, regardless of how much influence he had.

But there was no proof whatsoever that the brewery manager had ordered Hans to be kidnaped, and without such proof the *Swedish Daily Journal* would not be willing to publicize the issue.

The journalist was just about to present his conclusions to Jan when he realized that Jan's facial expression was one of absolute confidence in Mr. Hammar's ability to help him out. Having tried every other possibility, he felt that the reporter was his last and final hope. Mr. Hammar was quiet for a moment, and then he made clear to Jan that there might be nothing he could do, but if there were any way to help, he would certainly follow it.

After Jan had gone, the reporter sat for a while pondering

what he had heard, finally coming to the conclusion that it
would be shameful to sit idly by. So, in spite of the fact that
he had come to Bangkok merely as a tourist, he decided to do
a little research on the Nittel case. The first thing he did was
to have the hotel clerk cancel his reservation on the Scandinavian Airlines' flight the following day. Then he dressed
and rode out in a taxi to the installation. From there the
journalist made his way to the Austrian Embassy, finally paying a call on the chief of police. All he knew about the case
was what had been told him by a young boy who was himself
deeply involved in the events. The journalist realized that it
was his duty to check to see if the boy had been telling the
story straight. It turned out, actually, as he thought it would
from the start: Jan had told him the full story without any
embellishments of his own.

That afternoon Mr. Hammar took a taxi to Bangkok's
Chamber of Commerce to get more information about the
brewery and its owner. He also called at the Ministry of
Health, where a very helpful clerk gave him a ministry bro-
chure, on page 59 of which was the following, in English:

> "Tap water these days is completely drinkable, but old su-
> perstitions die hard, and the population still holds to the
> custom of boiling their drinking water before use. They
> also use 'Green Spot' and other soft drinks, which are on
> sale everywhere. 'Green Spot' and 'Bireley' are noncar-
> bonated."

Accustomed as he was to propaganda brochures and their
exaggerations, he felt that these few lines told him more than
enough.

In addition, the reporter called on the editor of one of the Thailand daily papers, where he made the acquaintance of a colleague who was not only charming and helpful in every way but also very well informed about local affairs. Mr. Hammar invited him to dinner and, without having to reveal why he was so interested in the matter, got a lot of valuable information about the brewery manager and his many political connections in high places.

While he went about collecting information, and taxiing from place to place, he had the constant feeling that he was being followed. Again and again he turned around in his seat in the small yellow three-wheeled vehicle, trying to discover if someone were shadowing him, but the traffic was so heavy that it was impossible to tell whether or not he was being followed. Every time he left a place, he looked around cautiously, but for a European who is not used to Asians, it was difficult to tell their faces apart. Still, all the while he sensed that he was being observed, a feeling that grew stronger as he ate dinner at the restaurant with his journalist friend.

The next morning Jan stopped in at his hotel, this time accompanied by Snit. He explained that Snit had been so discouraged the previous day that Jan felt he had to tell him about his meeting with Mr. Hammar in order to cheer him up a little. The young Thai lad seemed deep in gloom, but the expression in his eyes was so expectant that the reporter felt, more than ever, it was his duty to help them. Both faces lighted up with joy when Mr. Hammar told them of his investigations the previous day, but when he admitted that he hadn't been able to unearth any proof against the brewery manager, their hearts sank.

"It seems to me the only possibility is to make Scarface tell what he knows," said Snit.

The three of them decided to go to the police chief and ask to talk with the arrested police lieutenant. But they were forced to return from headquarters with their mission unac-

complished. The chief told them politely but firmly that it
was against all rules to allow anyone but the defense attorney
and the prosecution to talk with the accused. There was nothing to do. The reporter returned to the hotel for lunch and
the boys went home to eat, but before parting, they agreed to
meet in the lobby of the hotel when the early afternoon rain
was over.

After lunch Mr. Hammar went up to his air-conditioned
room in an attempt to escape the heat. Soon the noise of the
air-conditioning machine had lulled him to sleep, but half
an hour later the porter called to say that the younger Mr.
Grundvahl wanted to see him at once. Something very important must have happened.

When Mr. Hammar reached the lobby, he saw Jan, with
perspiration streaming from his forehead but with a joyful
expression on his face. His eyes shone, and he was smiling.

"Hans is back, Mr. Hammar. He's at our house right now,
eating lunch." The words tumbled from his mouth. "Thanks
a thousand million times. We all thank you. Now, you've got
to come home with us and meet Hans so that he can thank
you, too."

Mr. Hammar asked the porter to get them a taxi; they tied
Jan's bicycle to the baggage rack and drove to the Grundvahl
house. On the way Jan reported that Hans was well and that
he had seemed in good health when he returned. The brewery
manager's men had held him prisoner in a suburban villa.
Jan continued to emphasize their gratitude for all the "help"
Mr. Hammar had given them, and the reporter managed to
squeeze in a question as to what Jan meant by all this talk.
Actually, he had done nothing more than concern himself in
the matter, he said, and try to get a little information about it.

"Yes, but that's exactly what did the trick!" Jan explained with deep conviction. "I knew that I was being followed everywhere right after I left the brewery manager's office. In the evening, my daytime shadow was replaced by a new man who stood on watch across the street from our house, and every time I looked out the window, even in the middle of the night, I saw the man standing at his station behind the lamp post out there. They continued to shadow me the next day, and yesterday, when I came to the hotel, a car was trailing me the whole time. Maybe you didn't notice that a man followed me into the dining room yesterday and sat down at a table a little distance away, but he did, and all the time we were talking he kept his eyes glued on us. After that he followed you instead of me. I'm pretty sure that he was right on your heels all day yesterday."

"Very possible," Mr. Hammar answered. "I can't really say for sure, but all the while I felt that I was being followed. But why do you think we were shadowed?"

"Oh," Jan said cheerfully, "anyone can tell that you don't read detective stories. He, or rather they—because I am sure that at least two men were on the job—were underlings of the brewery manager. Obviously, he wanted to keep track of what I did and who I was in touch with. You see, he couldn't be absolutely positive that I didn't have an ace up my sleeve in spite of everything. And when he found out that I had seen you and that you were taking the matter seriously, he was naturally afraid that the thing would break into the press all over the world, which is why he let Hans go. So you, Mr. Hammar, were the one who really rescued Hans."

At the villa, the reporter met Mr. and Mrs. Grundvahl, Mr. and Mrs. Grimes, and the Freckles boys. Snit greeted him as he would a long-lost friend. He found Hans to be a very nice young man. Clearly, he was in a festive mood and seemed to be in good condition. He told them that the Sunday of his disappearance he was sitting at the installation office all alone when a car with two well-dressed Thailanders drove up to the entrance. One of the men introduced himself as a representative of the Ministry of Health and asked for some information, as well as for permission to look at the installation.

"Naturally, I invited them in and showed them the plant," he continued. "After the tour, I invited them into the office, in accordance with the Thailand custom, and offered them each a cup of green tea. I fixed a cup for myself, of course, and I guess while my back was turned one of them put some sort of powder in it. As soon as I had drunk it, I felt fuzzy in the head and so weak that I almost fell off my chair. Then one of my guests offered to help me get out into the fresh air and escorted me to their car. By that time I was almost unconscious and was, therefore, unable to put up a struggle."

"And they were the ones who took the typewriter with them," Snit added.

"That's right. When I came to, I was in a strange room, and the first thing I remember was their putting a pen in my hand, telling me that I had to write my signature on a piece of paper. One of them said this was so I could be admitted to the hospital since I had some sort of tropical fever."

And that was the story of Hans's disappearance and the subsequent letter to Mr. Grimes. He went on to say that the house where he had been held looked rather unlived in but that at all times he had been guarded by at least three men. They had provided him with everything he needed—including books and newspapers—but they were careful to see to it that he had no contact with the outside world, and since all three of them were armed, it was hopeless to try and get away. One of the three had told him that he had nothing to fear and that as soon as his disappearance was a forgotten matter, they would arrange for his transportation to North Viet Nam, where they were in great need of engineers and where he would consequently fare very well. He had never laid eyes on Scarface, nor, for that matter, the brewery manager. Maybe Scarface had been telling the truth when he said he knew nothing at all about Hans's disappearance because it was not at all impossible that the kidnaping had taken place without his knowledge—pulled off, perhaps, by other underlings of the brewery manager.

Later that afternoon Hans accompanied Mr. Grimes and Mr. Grundvahl on a visit to the chief of police, who was visibly happy to see him again and who listened carefully to all he had to say. In the company of two detectives, Hans was sent out to try to locate the house where he had been held, and after a couple of hours they found it. By that time, of course, the house was completely empty, and there were no signs whatsoever that Hans and the three guards had been there as recently as the day before. All the furniture was gone, the lock had been changed, and a little dust had even been scattered on the floor so that it would look as if no one had been there for several months.

In the evening they all celebrated Hans's return with a wonderful party at the Grundvahl home, featuring a genuine Swedish smörgåsbord with twenty different delicacies, and the next morning Lars Hammar boarded a Scandinavian Airlines' plane to Tokyo. He filed no story on the Bangkok episode, but that was of little consequence. After Hans had been freed, the whole business had taken on an unreal quality, and the liberation of one person was worth more than all the sensational journalism in the world.

Several weeks later, Mr. Hammar, back in Stockholm following his jaunt to Japan, received a very detailed letter from Jan, telling everything that had happened since the reporter had departed.

Mrs. Grimes and the Freckles boys had gone home to the United States in time for the new school year, and Hans and Mr. Grimes had returned to work at the installation. For the time being, Snit was living out there once more, working as night watchman together with Mikki, formerly Dog, and Jan was helping out daily, as well.

"But the summer is nearly over now and the new term is almost here. I will be attending a British private school in Bangkok," Jan said, concluding his long, interesting letter in a tone of melancholy. In line with this, Snit was going to quit his job at the installation, because, on the recommendation of Mr. Grundvahl, he had been accepted at a technical school in Bangkok where there were courses for both technicians and mechanics. Snit had said that he was thinking about learning hydraulic boring and following in the footsteps of Mr. Grimes.

Just a week later came still another letter from Bangkok, saying that Scarface had been sentenced to five years in prison and also that the brewery manager had been arrested and was now in the custody of the police. No doubt he had gone so far outside the law in some of his activities that even his millions and his many friends could no longer come to his rescue.

There was something else in Jan's letter—a photograph

he had taken himself. It was a picture of a tall, powerful stream of water against the background of the barrack, with a smiling, happy Hans to the left of the stream.

"Our first well. Chapter Two follows soon," was the legend on the back of the snapshot.

Lars Hammar kept the picture, and every time he looked at it, he experienced a certain feeling of pride—because, one way or another, even he had contributed to the project of bringing to the friendly, happy people of Bangkok pure, fresh drinking water for which they would not have to pay.